"Get Out Of My Room, Cole Garrett Tremaine!"

Cole laughed at Chelsea. "Well, you're back to normal—normal for you being feisty, outspoken and rebellious."

"It's a necessity when it comes to dealing with the likes of you."

"But I prefer women docile, submissive and compliant," he replied silkily. "And you'll be all of those things once this little vacation in the mountains is over."

"Never." Chelsea knew her words were bolder than her actions could ever be. She almost blushed when she remembered the passionate kisses they'd once shared. "I am curious about one thing, Cole. Why did you tell me the truth about bringing me here? Wouldn't it have been easier to pretend you wanted me back . . . and *then* laugh in my face?"

"Tricking you would have been too easy, Chelsea. Since I've given you fair warning, your unconditional surrender will be far more satisfying."

Dear Reader:

Welcome to Silhouette Desire—sensual, compelling, believable love stories written by and for today's woman. When you open the pages of a Silhouette Desire, you open yourself up to a whole new world—a world of promising passion and endless love.

Each and every Silhouette Desire is a wonderful love story that is both sensuous *and* emotional. You're with the hero and heroine each and every step of the way—from their first meeting, to their first kiss . . . to their happy ending. You'll experience all the deep joys—and occasional tribulations—of falling in love.

In future months, look for Silhouette Desire novels from some of your favorite authors, such as Naomi Horton, Nancy Martin, Linda Lael Miller and Lass Small, just to name a few.

So go wild with Desire. You'll be glad you did!

Lucia Macro
Senior Editor

BARBARA BOSWELL

ANOTHER WHIRLWIND COURTSHIP

Published by Silhouette Books New York
America's Publisher of Contemporary Romance

SILHOUETTE BOOKS
300 East 42nd St., New York, N.Y. 10017

ISBN: 0-373-05583-8

First Silhouette Books printing August 1990

Printed in the U.S.A.

Books by Barbara Boswell

Silhouette Desire

Rule Breaker #558
Another Whirlwind Courtship #583

BARBARA BOSWELL

loves writing about families. "I guess family has been a big influence on my writing," she says. "I particularly enjoy writing about how my characters' family relationships affect them."

When Barbara isn't writing and reading, she's spending time with her *own* family—her husband, three daughters and three cats, who she concedes are the true bosses of their home! She has lived in Europe, but now makes her home in Pennsylvania. She collects miniatures, holiday ornaments, tries to avoid exercise and has somehow found the time to write over twenty category romances.

One

Chelsea Kincaid had just pulled her trusty blue Honda into the passing lane when she first noticed that something seemed to be wrong. Her car was definitely veering to the right. Her knowledge of auto maintenance and repair was not great, but she refused to accept that anything might be seriously wrong.

There simply couldn't be a problem. Not while she was driving west on Interstate 70 at a speed far exceeding her usual cautious rate. Not while she was escaping from the city of Washington, D.C., where, until two hours ago, she'd been scheduled to marry the son of the President of the United States in a lavish ceremony. A ceremony that was to take place on the White House lawn in the full presence of the worldwide press.

Chelsea thought of the battalions of news hounds both in the electronic and print media who had joined forces to turn this White House wedding into an epochal extravaganza.

The entire horde would also be on hand to transform the sudden cancellation into an epochal debacle....

The right front side of the car began to dip ominously and it became more difficult to keep the car straight. No, Chelsea assured herself, the tire could not be losing air. It wouldn't dare go flat. She could not be, she *would* not be, stuck on the interstate with a flat tire at the precise moment that she was supposed to have been exchanging vows with Seth Strickland amidst orange blossoms and video cameras.

For just a moment, she permitted herself to think about the media circus masquerading as a wedding, with herself thrust into the unwilling role of bride. Chelsea Kincaid, the Hapless Bride. The Horrified Bride. That was her. Hardly the image of the stars-in-her-eyes bride packaged by the Strickland White House and perpetrated by the press.

But then, her mistake of a relationship with Seth was hardly the modern-day fairy tale concocted by the media, Chelsea acknowledged grimly. It was a ghastly error in judgment blown completely out of proportion by a romance-hungry press that had hounded her since her first date three months ago with the new President's handsome, eligible son.

Dubbed the "First Wedding," theirs was to have been a nuptial event to rival those of the British royal family. The press and public seemed ravenous for details, no matter how trivial. Seth and his mother Georgia, the gregarious and ever-youthful First Lady, made the rounds of every talk show to discuss the plans and particulars; occasionally the President himself joined them. Nobody seemed to care that the bride-to-be wasn't along or that during her rare public appearances, she remained practically mute. When the dashing bridegroom-to-be described his future bride as "shy," the entire country believed him.

And now...Chelsea shivered. Heaven only knew what they would say about her now. When she'd called Seth earlier this morning to inform him of her decision to cancel the wedding, she'd left it to him and the Strickland public relations staff to release whatever statement they wanted about the abrupt change of plans. She hadn't turned on the car radio to find out what they'd come up with. Whatever they said, she would agree with, she vowed. Didn't she owe the Stricklands that much?

The right front end of the car was now sagging so low it seemed to be hitting the ground. Gripping the wheel tightly, Chelsea used all her strength to steer the car onto the shoulder, as far from traffic as she could get, and parked under the shade of an overhanging tree. Her worst suspicions were confirmed when she viewed the troublesome right front tire. It was losing air so swiftly that within the next few moments, it would be completely flat.

She groaned. "Now what?" she asked out loud. She knew she had a spare in the trunk, but she had never changed a tire in her life.

Tiny pinpricks of heat stabbed in her head. She grimaced. Though it was midmorning and already hazy, hot and humid, Chelsea knew the June weather was not responsible for those little staccato darts in her temple. She had a history of migraine headaches, and though their frequency had diminished over the years by following doctors' recommendations, the headaches had returned with a vengeance during this three-month siege with Seth Strickland. Although she'd avoided caffeine and hadn't missed any meals, stress could bring on a migraine—and Seth and the First Wedding plans were prime stressors.

She knew only too well from past experience that the tiny needles of heat in her temples were a sign that a migraine was developing. No, Chelsea silently raged, she would *not* have one, not now! She would will the potential headache away and send the contributing stress along with it. After all, she reasoned, there were worse things than being stranded along the interstate with a flat tire in the hot summer sun while fleeing the wrath of Seth and the Stricklands.

She could be marrying Seth Strickland under a canopy on the White House lawn.

A chill crept through her as Seth's voice, a loud enraged screech echoed in her ears. "You can't do this to me!" he'd bellowed when she had informed him that the wedding was off. He'd called her an assortment of names, none of which could be printed in a family newspaper. But it was what he hadn't said that completely justified her decision to herself. While he'd ranted about public embarrassment and inconvenience, he had never once mentioned that he loved her and she was breaking his heart. Because they'd never loved each other outside of the media spotlight, they'd never even pretended to.

Seth Strickland didn't love her, but that wouldn't stop him from seeking vengeance because she'd screwed up his plans to be First Groom. Once again his threat rebounded in her brain: "You won't get away with this. We Stricklands haven't gotten as far as we have by letting people make fools of us. You're going to marry me whether you want to or not. I'll force you if I have to, I'll do whatever it takes to make you go through with this damn wedding."

The menace in his tone had galvanized Chelsea into flight. Until then, she'd been prepared to ride out the negative storm of publicity, to take whatever the press dished out, to go on with her life and career as a writer for the D.C.-based magazine *Capitol Scene*. But the appalling prospect of a forced wedding sent her running. Marriage was scary enough as a voluntary act; a compulsory marriage was a theme for a horror story.

Her parents' bitter divorce, which had fueled her own lifelong uncertainties and fears of marriage, served as terrifying evidence of love turned to hate. She and her younger sister Stefanie had been used as weapons by their battling parents for the past twenty years, long after each had remarried and started new families with new mates.

Chelsea thought of the pledge that she and Stefanie had made over and over again through the years; the vow to never, ever end up in a miserable marriage followed by a vitriolic divorce.

She thought back to Seth's threat. *I'll do whatever it takes to make you go through with this damn wedding.* Panicking, Chelsea had impulsively thrown some things into her suitcase and taken off.

Suppose the Stricklands were to use the full force of presidential power against her. The prospect was truly hair-raising. The small throbs in her head sharpened and intensified.

A big, black stretch limousine with darkly tinted windows suddenly swerved off the highway to pull onto the shoulder several yards behind her. Her already soaring anxiety level leapt into the stratosphere. Chelsea watched with a kind of fascinated horror as the front door on the driver's side of the car swung open. Her heartbeat thudded in her ears as she waited to see who would emerge.

A wrathful Seth Strickland? A scoop-seeking band of reporters? At this moment, even the appearance of a murderous hit man burnishing an assault rifle—compliments of Commander-in-Chief Walter Strickland—seemed possible.

But the tall, broad-shouldered, muscular man striding toward her didn't belong in any of those categories. Chelsea instantly recognized him, even though his face was partially masked by his mirrored sunglasses. She would have known that strong build, the thick, straight blackness of his hair, that rangy male stride of his anywhere, anytime.

He was Cole Garrett Tremaine.

Chelsea was unable to suppress her audible gasp of shock at the sight of him. For one perilous moment, she was certain she would faint. Cole, her first love, her first lover... and briefly, her first fiancée. Here, now. It was too bizarre to be coincidental, yet impossible to be anything else.

She'd last seen him four years ago, on that fateful day she'd broken their engagement, just hours before it was to have been officially announced at a big party in their honor.

"I can't believe it's you!" she burst out, nearly breathless with astonishment. Inhaling deeply, she tried hard to gain some semblance of control. "I—I was driving and then the tire went flat and so I had to—" She broke off, flushing. Even to her own ears, she sounded as if she were babbling. And suddenly, she was too flustered to speak at all.

Cole had stopped walking and stood stock still, his arms folded in front of his chest, his stance wide as he watched her. His impeccably tailored navy pin-striped suit added to his aura of command and authority. Even standing along the roadside, he maintained the image of forceful executive and scion of a wealthy, powerful family. A few months shy of thirty-five, he was already general counsel and vice president of Tremaine Incorporated, the holding company of his family's chain of area discount drugstores and national chain of bookstores. It was no secret in the business world that he would succeed his father, Richard Tremaine, as head of the company upon the older man's retirement.

Stunned and shaken, Chelsea stared at him and swallowed, hard.

"Surprised to see me?" Cole drawled.

His voice seemed to flow over her like warm honey. It was the first time she'd heard it in four years. The sound brought back scorching memories of whispers in the heat of passion, of urgent hungry demands and husky avowals of love.

Her knees went weak and she was bombarded by the barrage of memories of him, which always seemed to be lurking in the back of her mind....

Four years ago she had loved Cole Tremaine more than she'd ever dreamed it possible to love anyone. But rushing into marriage on the heels of a passionate whirlwind courtship had seemed incredibly foolhardy to her. She'd heard all about her parents' impetuous wedding, and had lived with their bitterness and regret her entire life. Kincaid family history dictated that a whirlwind courtship that culminated in marriage wasn't romantic. It was *disastrous*. Cole hadn't shared her trepidations. To him love and marriage were inextricably linked, and time was not a factor.

She'd tried to make him see that they hadn't known each other long enough, that there were still too many unresolved issues between them that needed to be ironed out before marriage, not after it. She *needed* time, she'd pleaded. They both did.

Cole hadn't agreed. Chelsea was deeply in love with him, but she'd refused to set a wedding date in the near future as Cole had demanded. So he had ended their relationship. Permanently. She could still remember how cold and hard his blue eyes were when he'd finally said, "You win. It's over."

But Chelsea had known, as she'd felt her heart breaking, that she hadn't won anything. She had lost Cole's love and her dreams of their future together. Although she believed she had made the right decision by not rushing into marriage, it was cold consolation. Why did being right have to feel so terribly wrong? And while one part of her missed him, yearned for him, another part of her hated him for leaving her so easily, so irrevocably.

"I've been watching you wrestle with the car for the past five miles," Cole continued coolly. "Why didn't you pull off the road sooner? Don't you know that riding on the rim causes irreparable damage to it and the tire?"

Chelsea gaped at him, bereft of speech. Cole had always possessed an unnerving talent for scrambling her thoughts. He'd just done it again. She didn't know which of his points to consider first—that he'd been following her for at least five miles or that she was an incompetent driver who needed a lecture on tire safety?

"Nothing to say?" Cole remarked dryly. "I know we've all heard the old adage 'silence is golden,' but you seem bent on carrying it to extremes these days. You appeared to be bordering on catatonia during Seth Strickland's exuberant First Courtship. The only words the country has heard you speak was your name during that exclusive TV interview with Barbara Walters. Luckily Seth and his loquacious mama were there to pick up the slack. You sat there looking like a prisoner of war. I wouldn't have been surprised if you'd given rank and serial number after your name and signaled SOS by blinking your eyes."

A sardonic half-smile twisted the corners of his mouth. Chelsea knew that behind his concealing mirrored sunglasses, his dark blue eyes, piercing and intense, were undoubtedly gleaming with mockery as well.

"I don't want to talk about it," she murmured, her cheeks flaming.

"What don't you want to talk about, Chelsea? That embarrassing interview? Or the fact that you left Seth Strickland standing at the altar?"

"I didn't!" She looked at the ground and bit her lower lip. "Not *literally* standing at the altar." Her voice lowered. "I called this morning to tell him that—that the wedding was off."

"How thoughtful of you to give him a few hours notice!" Cole shook his head and laughed disparagingly. "I guess I should consider myself lucky. Being dumped shortly before an engagement party for friends and family is infinitely preferable to being jilted a few hours before an internationally televised wedding.

"Can you guess what's going to be the lead story in the news tonight?" he continued with jovial derision. "And this is one media event that the publicity-loving Stricklands would prefer not to have a starring role in."

Chelsea winced. "I said I don't want to talk about it, Cole," she said tightly. To stress her disapproval, she subjected him to her most intimidating glare, guaranteed to quell any upstart.

Cole, however, was neither intimidated nor quelled. "What? You don't want to revel in all your headlining glory? I hope you've employed a clipping service, Chelsea. There will be accounts of the aborted First Wedding in newspapers and magazines all over the world. Maybe you can paste them in a scrapbook. It'll make quite a souvenir."

Chelsea's nerves were jangling. She was flushed and tense, and that knowing smile of Cole's proclaimed that he was thoroughly enjoying her discomfiture. A bolstering anger rallied her. "Your nasty little jokes aren't the least bit amusing. You sound like a heartless, unfeeling cynic who—"

"Oh no!" Cole feigned dismay. "Call me anything, but not a heartless, unfeeling cynic!" He grinned broadly, clearly enjoying himself at her expense.

Chelsea seethed. "You can go straight to hell, Cole Tremaine!"

He arched his dark brows. "No thanks, I've already been there, four years ago after you worked me over. I don't care to make a return trip—now it's Strickland's turn. As for being heartless, unfeeling and cynical... well, I wasn't always, as we both know."

"It was your choice to become a slick, arrogant smooth operator, Cole Tremaine. Don't you dare try to blame me."

She'd intended to insult him. Instead he laughed, clearly delighted. "Slick, arrogant smooth operator, huh? Me?"

"It's not a compliment," she said stonily. "It's sickening the way your name is always appearing in the gossip columns with all those women."

"I've learned a lot about women since my days as a nice guy with you, Chelsea. The first lesson was that the cliché 'nice guys finish last' is right on target. The heartbreakers with their aura of risk and sexual danger are the men that women really want."

"You don't actually believe that sexist garbage!" Chelsea was appalled.

"It's become the credo that I live by, darling. Women say one thing and mean another. They don't respect a man who is honest and open with them. A man must keep a woman off-balance and never let her know what he really feels."

So many outraged replies, retorts and rejoinders sprang to her mind, that it was difficult to choose which one to blast him with first. She was profoundly shocked by the change in him. The Cole Tremaine she had known and loved had been quiet, serious and dedicated to his career with Tremaine Incorporated, not to the Washington social scene. But since their breakup, he'd turned into a regular man-about-town who never missed a party. His dates ran the gamut from Brandi, the bubble-gum chewing starlet to Martha, the state supreme court judge.

Somehow, Chelsea had kept track of them all, feeling an odd sense of relief when none of the relationships turned into anything lasting. That is, until his latest one, his rumored "serious involvement" with Senator Clayton Templeton's beautiful daughter Carling. Chelsea had learned about it just days before she'd been introduced to Seth Strickland at the Bulgarian Embassy party she'd been covering for *Capitol Scene*. That had been three fateful months ago.

"Anyway, when it comes to having your name bandied about all over town, you royally outdid me, baby," Cole taunted, robbing her of the opportunity to slap down his outrageous claims. "Yours has been plastered over the whole country. I could hardly believe it when I heard that you were dating Seth Strickland. And all this First Wedding nonsense..."

His voice trailed off and he scowled. The sickeningly cute media tag had a visceral effect upon him. When he'd first heard the announcement of Chelsea and Seth Strickland's upcoming marriage, he'd actually had to sit down and catch his breath. He'd felt as if he'd been punched in the gut.

He was feeling that way now. The sight of Chelsea could still send him reeling, even after four years apart. Four years....

Four years ago he had been obsessed with her. Just twenty-three then, seven and a half years younger than himself, Chelsea Kincaid had been an irresistible, fascinating mixture of feminine contrasts. A sweet, serious graduate student with an angel's face and a lively intelligence who also possessed a pair of dark, dreamy eyes, a sexy mane of dark red hair and the seductive body of a centerfold pinup. Equally compelling was her fiery, passionate temperament, which she determinedly reined in with controlled calm. Sometimes. He had always been able to break through her defenses and free her passion, both in and out of bed.

For one brief moment, Cole allowed himself to remember those days, when he had been so intensely, obsessively in love with her. Never had he experienced such powerful emotions, not before nor since his whirlwind courtship of Chelsea Anne Kincaid. The memories washed over him.

He had been the rising star in the legal department of Tremaine Incorporated the summer he'd met Chelsea. She was one of his younger brother Nathaniel's grad school classmates who had been invited to the Tremaines for an end-of-the-term celebratory pool party.

She had been standing on the diving board, shapely and stunning in a sea-green maillot, her red hair pulled high in a long, thick braid, when Cole first saw her. The image was seared indelibly in his mind's eye. And then she'd executed the worst dive he'd ever seen, hitting the water in an ignominious belly flop. Laughing, he'd introduced himself and offered a few diving tips.

Their attraction was mutual and strong and progressed rapidly, passionately into something deeper and more intense. Before Chelsea, Cole had invested the major portion of his energy, passion and interest in his career. But with her, everything was different. For the first time, his personal life took precedence over his work. Within weeks he'd wanted, *demanded* the exclusivity and commitment that only marriage could provide. He wanted to possess her in every way. He wanted her to have his children. He loved her; she belonged to him.

Like a deluded idiot, he had believed she loved him, too. Right up until the day she had broken their engagement. That unpleasant memory immediately jarred him out of his reverie. Cole's scowl deepened. And now here they stood four years later, on the very day that she'd run out on her wedding to another man.

Two

A taut, tense silence stretched between them. Chelsea was the first to break it. "I haven't heard the Stricklands' official announcement," she said nervously, deciding to try another tack. Trading insults with him was not going well; her retaliatory efforts were woefully lacking. "When did they announce that the wedding was canceled?" Her big, brown eyes were as round as saucers. "How did they...explain it?"

Cole shrugged. "I haven't heard any official announcement. I don't think one has been issued yet."

Chelsea's jaw dropped. "Then how did you know that—"

"I saw you leave your apartment," Cole interjected coolly. His eyes flicked over her, taking in her comfortably baggy white shorts, her oversize purple-and-white shirt, her socks and sneakers. Her thick auburn hair was pulled high into a ponytail from which wisps were already escaping. "You sure as hell weren't dressed for a wedding and you headed out of the city. I drew the obvious conclusion."

Chelsea tried and failed to suppress a gasp. "You've been following me since I left Washington?" It wasn't possible, she assured herself. His arrival had to be coincidental. He was merely trying to unnerve her—and he was succeeding masterfully, she silently admitted.

Cole shrugged again. "Drove by your apartment building this morning and saw you slip into your car with your suitcase. Poor Strickland." He laughed without mirth. "I almost feel sorry for him. Even if he is a smug, self-satisfied creep with an ego three times the size of China."

"Four times the size of China," Chelsea corrected grimly.

"Is that why you did it, Chelsea? To knock him down a peg or two?"

"Of course not!" she snapped. "What kind of a person do you think I am?"

Cole smiled a fake smile, showing his even white teeth. "Do you really want me to answer that, Chelsea?"

Chelsea's face burned. "No, I really do not." She launched a quick, cool offensive of her own. "I want you to tell me why you're here, dressed like a corporate executive for a meeting with the board of directors and driving a limousine bigger than a hearse."

"I'm dressed for a wedding, sweetheart. Yours. My official engraved invitation, complete with presidential seal, is in the car. So considerate of you to invite me."

"I didn't invite you!" Chelsea was aghast. "I had no idea that—"

"The invitation was issued from the Strickland guest list. While he's not exactly an insider, my dad has known Walt Strickland for years. Our whole family was invited, but I was the only one who was actually going to go. Carling wanted to, so I took the company limo for the occasion."

Carling. Just hearing the name on his lips stirred an intensely primitive response within Chelsea. She fought to appear nonchalant. "Carling Templeton?" She hoped her tone conveyed the indifference she was *not* experiencing.

"How many other Carlings do you know?"

"None. And I don't even know her. I only met her once at a party with Seth. I—heard you two were serious." There, she'd said it. Chelsea balled her hands into fists and braced herself for his response.

"Did you?" He smiled again, that fixed baring-of-teeth which was as far from a real smile as giggling was from sobbing.

Chelsea gritted her teeth. Let it drop, she counseled herself, but she was infamous for not taking her own good advice and instead blurted out, "Well, are you?"

"Are Carling and I seriously involved?" Cole paused, as if carefully considering the question. Then he said briskly, "Call me antisocial, but I don't care to stand around swapping romantic confidences with my former fiancée. Besides, we've wasted enough time talking." He strode past her to open the left door of her car and removed her suitcase from the small backseat.

Chelsea cringed in the throes of embarrassment. How coolly he'd avoided her blatant probing! But the sight of her suitcase in his hand replaced her humiliation with a chilling realization. He must have watched her put the bag in the car to know exactly where to find it now. Her coincidence theory, which she had grasped onto, was finally blown to smithereens. "You really *did* see me leave my apartment!" she exclaimed. "You really *have* been following me."

"You really have a remarkable grasp of the obvious," he drawled.

His condescending tone inflamed her. "Why did you drive past my apartment this morning?" she demanded.

"To check and see if the wedding was on or off." He shrugged diffidently. "You see, I was invited to a pre-wedding brunch and I was asked to bring the Bloody Marys. I thought I'd make sure it was necessary before I went to the trouble of whipping up a batch. And I'm glad I did. I'd have been stuck with gallons of the stuff."

She was almost too flabbergasted to speak. "What made you think I might call off the wedding?" she managed at last. "I didn't know if I would do it, if I *could* do it, until late last night." Following hours of soul-searching and pacing. She hadn't slept at all.

"Call it intuition, if you will. Remember, I once had the dubious privilege of being engaged, however briefly, to you. I'm well acquainted with the convolutions of your tormented psyche. Why do you do it, Chelsea? Why do you keep getting yourself engaged to men you don't want to marry?"

The carelessness in his voice, the casual sarcasm, sent her temper rocketing. "Perhaps the question ought to be why do men insist on rushing me to the altar! Seth never *asked* me to marry him, he *told* me he was going to marry me—*after* he told his father's press secretary to release the news. I tried not to panic, I told Seth that I had no intention of being pressured into a quickie wedding. I even told him that I didn't love him!"

"Let me guess," Cole said dryly. "Seth of the Incredible Ego suggested that you really did love him but you just hadn't realized it yet."

"He suggested that eventually we could learn to love each other," Chelsea corrected grimly. "He went full-steam ahead with the wedding plans. He got his mother involved and then everything happened so fast I was swept along like a piece of flotsam in a flood. I tried talking to the Stricklands but they kept misinterpreting everything I said. It was maddening! All they could talk about was the publicity value and the historic significance of a wedding in the White House. How the children must be born right in the Lincoln bedroom—they even had the name of a midwife who agreed to deliver them there! I felt like a prop in a play they were staging. I knew that somehow I had to get out."

"So you did, with your usual superb flair for timing."

"I didn't deliberately stage this!" Chelsea was outraged. "Oh, why am I even trying to explain it to *you*, of all people! When we were engaged, you cast me in a role in your own private play just like Seth did. And when I wouldn't act out my assigned part you couldn't dump me fast enough."

"*I* dumped *you*?" Cole was incredulous. "Don't try to rewrite history, baby. I didn't back out of our engagement just as the caterers were arriving to set up for the big announcement party. I wasn't the one who refused to set a wedding date. You were."

"You expected me to do what you wanted when you wanted me to do it, without any discussion, questions or suggestions on my part." Frustration surged through her. "That isn't marriage, it's subservience! Marriage is teamwork with two equal partners making decisions together, not a master who manipulates and dominates his supplicant."

"I see you're still casting me as a chauvinistic tyrant simply because I wanted a wife and kids." He laughed caustically. "Yeah, that was reprehensible of me, wasn't it? Wanting to make a commitment, to have a family. How villainous can a man get?"

"This is the same argument we had four years ago!" Chelsea exclaimed. The emotions roiling within her suddenly heated to flashpoint. "And you still refuse to understand that I loved you and wanted to get married and have a family *eventually* but—"

"If you had really loved me it wouldn't have been *but* it would've been *therefore*, Chelsea. The truth is that everything and everybody else ran a poor second to your selfish and grandiose career ambitions."

Her brown eyes flashed fire. "I was working as a graduate assistant in the English department and writing the thesis required for my master's degree. I had less than a year to go and I wanted to finish before I got married. I still haven't figured out what is selfish or grandiose about that."

"What did it matter if you dropped out of the university? A master's degree was irrelevant to your future and so was a job." Cole's voice rose in exasperation. "I showed you every single one of my financial statements, Chelsea. You knew you'd be marrying a rich man. As my wife you would never have to worry about finding a job, so why bother getting an advanced degree?"

"Why bother with an advanced degree?" Chelsea choked. "Suppose someone had said that to you? Don't bother going to law school, don't bother trying to make something of yourself because your father is rich and you'll never have to worry about finding a job that pays a living wage!"

Cole shifted uncomfortably. "That's different," he muttered, frowning.

"Different? How? Because you happen to be male? With that attitude, I hope you never have daughters. You'd raise them to be useless, airheaded parasites who—"

"I would not!"

"It's too bad you never had any sisters. Maybe then you wouldn't find the concept of a woman wanting to use her brains *and* her uterus so alien!"

"My mother was a full-time wife and mother who devoted her life to her family. She didn't want or need anything else."

As always, he stopped her cold by invoking his sainted mother. The late, beautiful Marnie Tremaine had been elevated to sainthood by her widowed husband, who had never remarried and who had raised their three sons to worship her as womankind's *beau ideal*.

Chelsea had once pointed out to Cole that his mother's tragic death in a car accident at the age of twenty-nine had cut short the woman's life and ambitions. Had Marnie Tremaine lived she might have very well gone on to further her education or seek some sort of career. But Cole had refuted that heretical notion with the fervor of one defending a sacred doctrine. Chelsea had realized then and there that a mere mortal couldn't tamper with a venerated legend.

"I want a wonderful, old-fashioned marriage just like my parents had," Cole continued loftily. "My wife won't ever have to work, I'll give her everything she wants. Just as I was willing to give you everything," he added, his voice turning cold.

"Except the only thing I really wanted," Chelsea cut in quietly. "Time to be sure of us and our relationship. We'd dated for less than six months, Cole. And I wasn't just killing time in school, waiting for something better to come along. I'd worked two or three jobs all through college and graduate school to cover my tuition and expenses. Finishing successfully was very important to me."

Just as before, part of him admired her dedication and determination while another part of him was irritated by it. He was accustomed to taking charge, of being deferred to. And to succeeding. His failure to marry Chelsea was the only time in his life he'd ever failed at anything. A surge of hot emotion ripped through him.

"So now you have your degree, which netted you a low-paying job on a struggling magazine." His angry smile mocked her. "You write two-line synopses of television programs for *Capitol Scene*. Any second thoughts about your glorious career, Chelsea?"

Fury slashed through her. Cole had a knack for hitting on what would rile her most. "If the pay is low, it's because there are scores of talented people vying to break into a writing career. The opportunities and experience that come with my position are invaluable. *Capitol Scene* is an excellent, respected magazine with a bright future. And I write more than TV promos. I've also—"

"You also review movies for *Capitol Scene.* You're assigned to the witless comedies and the teen slasher flicks because the magazine's pretentious drama critic always reviews the best films himself."

"You seem quite familiar with the magazine." Her voice dripped with acid sweetness. "And since you're such a faithful reader, you'll also know that I've also done a number of in-depth character profiles and investigative articles. My series on teenage pregnancy in the District was quoted in an article in *USA Today.*"

"Impressive. And what is your current job status, Chelsea? Did you intend to continue writing for the magazine as Seth Strickland's wife?"

She nodded. "But I'm not working on anything at the moment. In addition to my two-week paid vacation, I took an extra two weeks unpaid leave of absence."

"Ah, there's a new concept for the work place—debacle leave. Very innovative of you, Chelsea. But it was a pipe dream to think you could ever return to the magazine as First Daughter-in-law. You wouldn't be allowed to write anything remotely informative or controversial in that role, you know. The Stricklands would never agree to you doing anything but puff pieces, and they'd insist on approving any article before publication."

"I know," she said quietly. "That was just one of the many, many reasons why I knew it would never work out between Seth and me."

"Do you intend to write about your flight from the altar, Chelsea?" He couldn't seem to stop baiting her and he didn't bother to wonder why. "That should give *Capitol*

Scene a much-needed circulation boost. Every newspaper in the country will want to print excerpts from the notorious runaway bride's story. But we've wasted enough time talking." Still carrying her suitcase, he turned and strode purposefully toward the black limousine.

"What are you doing?" Chelsea demanded, following him.

He tossed the bag inside and turned, blocking her access to the open door, thus preventing her from retrieving the suitcase. "Get in the car, Chelsea," he ordered.

She stared at him. "What?"

"You're going with me." His voice was serious and commanding, the firm, compelling tones of the successful business attorney that he was.

"I don't understand." Chelsea backed away, her eyes wide with sudden alarm. Her voice reverberated in her head, like drums in an echo chamber.

"Then let me enlighten you. I'm kidnapping you."

Chelsea tried to tamp the wave of anxiety sweeping through her. "Don't be ridiculous, Cole."

Cole laughed, but it wasn't a pleasant sound. "I'm quite serious, darling. Now are you going to get in the car or shall I put you in?" he asked with feigned, overexaggerated politeness.

"I'm not doing anything until you tell me what you're up to." She glared at him, folding her arms in front of her chest in the classic defensive position. She was stalling for time, aware of sounding far more confident than she felt. Little stabs of heat grew red-hot along her scalp as she tried to think what to do next.

Her hesitation cost her the precious seconds she needed to beat a retreat to her own car. Before she could marshal her thoughts into some coherent plan of action, Cole was already on the move. He swung her off her feet and over his shoulder and carried her to the limousine, dumping her inside, then sliding in after her.

It happened with disorienting speed. One moment she was standing there, the next she was upside down. Cole's arms were gripping her like steel bands and she was being deposited into the front of the limo.

Stunned speechless, she scrambled toward the door and grabbed the handle. The door didn't open.

"Power locks," Cole said calmly, settling himself behind the wheel. "The master control is here, on my side."

"Let me out! You can't do this!" Chelsea found her voice, but to her dismay it sounded more like a breathless, high-pitched squeak.

"I'm doing it." Cole's voice, in contrast, was smooth and steady, without a trace of agitation. He gunned the engine and swiftly steered the limousine onto the interstate.

Chelsea turned to kneel on the seat and watch her car recede from view as the limousine sped away. The Honda looked forlorn and abandoned, with its useless, disabled tire.

"Sit down and fasten your seat belt, Chelsea," Cole ordered.

She didn't move. She couldn't move. Her thoughts whirled through her head, each leading to an ominous conclusion. He had followed her from the city and now... "Did you do something to my tire to make it go flat?" she whispered.

"Of course not. The flat tire was an unexpected but convenient coincidence."

"If it hadn't happened, how would you have—" she paused and gulped, "grabbed me? When I stopped for food or gas?"

He shrugged. "Sounds plausible, doesn't it?"

"Did the Stricklands send you?" A lump of fear lodged uncomfortably in her throat, making it difficult to talk.

"Do I strike you as a lackey that the Stricklands can dispatch at will?" Cole asked drolly.

She didn't know if it was a rhetorical question, but she answered it anyway. "No, but I heard that Tremaine Incorporated made a substantial financial contribution to Walter Strickland's presidential campaign last fall. You might be willing to do a—a personal favor for him, too."

"A personal favor like kidnapping son Seth's errant bride? Is that the way you believe politics work, Chelsea?" Cole flashed an insolent grin. "I'd like to hear what you think I should demand as payment for getting the fugitive bride to the church on time. A cabinet post? An ambassadorship? How about an appointment to the supreme court?"

"Cole, why are you doing this?" she cried wildly.

Good question, a mocking little voice in his head conceded. And what exactly was he doing? His mouth tightened. It was too difficult to admit to himself that he honestly didn't know, that he'd followed her on the spur of the moment, that "kidnapping" her was a spontaneous, irresistible impulse.

Why, it was unheard of! Anyone who knew Cole Tremaine knew that he never acted on impulse, never proceeded without a carefully thought out plan of action. He was calculating, cunning and shrewd and proud of it.

So why was he doing this? Cole asked himself. And if he managed to come up with a satisfactory answer to that question, there was another one he could work on: why had he impulsively stopped by his former fiancée's place on the morning of her wedding to another man in the first place?

The pre-wedding-brunch-and-Bloody-Mary tale he'd told her was pure fiction. Cole scowled. Then why *had* he gone there? To force himself to admit that Chelsea finally, truly belonged to another...or to prevent that from ever happening? He only knew that when he'd seen her slip furtively from the apartment, he had followed, instantly, instinctively, without a single conscious motive, scheme or reason in his head.

Now they were here, alone together, with her demanding why and suspecting him of the very sort of calculating, shrewd and cunning ploy that he had yet to come up with.

The silence stretched between them, unnerving her. Chelsea tried not to notice the jackhammer pain beginning to drill in her head. She had to concentrate on something else—such as why she was here. Since Cole refused to reply, she took a stab at answering her own question.

"For—for revenge?" she guessed, horror-stricken at the notion. "Is that why?"

Oh God, it couldn't be, she thought, panic surging through her. Her mother had always maintained that Cole had taken their breakup too well, that his subsequent behavior had been unbelievably, suspiciously free of reprisal. Her father had concurred; it was one of the few things Chelsea could ever remember her parents agreeing upon. Caught in a cycle of vengeance themselves, they couldn't comprehend anyone else not being equally driven by it.

Could her parents have been right? Chelsea wondered wildly. Had Cole merely been biding his time, waiting for the ideal opportunity to claim his revenge?

A cool smile curved Cole's lips. She had just provided him with a very satisfactory motive, scheme and reason, that fit handily into the calculating, shrewd and cunning image he enjoyed of himself. Yes, he was kidnapping her—for *revenge*!

"You've always been a quick study, Chelsea. Once again, you're right on target."

"Cole, no!" Still on her knees, she moved closer, placing an imploring hand on his arm. "Take me back to my car. Please let me go!" Her velvety brown eyes pleaded with him.

"It's not going to work, darling," he said in that caustic tone she was swiftly growing to hate. "The days when you could make me jump through hoops by batting those long, thick lashes of yours are long gone. I'm calling all the shots now."

"You always did," Chelsea countered, her cheeks flushing. "That was one of our biggest problems. Furthermore, I was *not* batting my eyelashes!"

"You were batting them like a simpering antebellum Southern miss, darling. Now sit down, buckle up and settle down."

"No! And stop calling me darling!"

"You used to love it when I called you darling. Or was that merely another one of your pretenses, like pretending that you loved me?"

"I never pretended! I really loved you! Why are you so unwilling or unable to believe that?"

"Maybe it has something to do with your refusal to marry me," Cole suggested derisively. "Oh, you didn't mind having me around on an unofficial basis. I was an older man with lots of money to spend on you, a rather prestigious catch for a struggling grad student. It was convenient for you to have a guaranteed date, you liked all the gifts I was forever buying you, and you enjoyed the places I could take you to. It was fun having a rich boyfriend, wasn't it, Chelsea? Until I started making all those tiresome demands for a commitment."

Chelsea burned. "Don't try to make me into some kind of conniving gold digger, Cole Tremaine! If I were, I'd have married you for your money. But I didn't and I—"

"You also used me for sex," Cole interrupted calmly, his face an impassive mask.

Chelsea didn't even try to suppress her gasp of outrage. She felt a primal, furious instinct to slap Cole before her rational, in-control self grimly took over again. She knew she should ignore him; she was at a great disadvantage, completely at his mercy. He was goading her for his own sport, to draw an irate response from her. She ought to deny him the pleasure. Still, she couldn't stay silent, disadvantage or not. He probably had no mercy anyway, not for her.

"I never used you for sex!" She hurled the words at him. "How dare you make such an insulting preposterous accusation?"

"I *dare* it because it happens to be the truth," he drawled laconically. "It seems I really hit a nerve, didn't I, Chelsea? We both know that I was the catalyst in your transformation from inhibited little virgin to sexy, passionate lover. You loved everything we did in bed. You couldn't get enough. You weren't interested in love and commitment but you didn't want to give up the sex. That's why you wanted to continue our relationship after you refused to marry me. You didn't love me, you loved a certain part of my anatomy and the pleasure it gave you."

"I don't have to passively sit here and listen to this!" Her eyes bright with fury, Chelsea abandoned her attempt at controlled rationality and reacted purely on impulse. "And I won't!" She lunged for the steering wheel. Catching him off guard, she managed to grab it with both hands and turn it sharply to the right.

"Take your hands off the wheel!" Cole shouted in alarm as the car careened off the road toward the shoulder.

"No!" snarled Chelsea, continuing to steer the car off the highway.

Cole relinquished the wheel, giving her control of the car. What choice did he have? Steering was not a job for two. Cursing, he applied the brakes slowly, as the car rolled onto the gravelly shoulder of the road. Finally, the big, black limousine ground safely to a halt.

His hands were trembling, and he quickly switched off the engine. "You crazy little idiot!" he bellowed. His heart was pounding and his whole body shaking as adrenaline surged through his veins. "That was the stupidest stunt I've ever seen! You could've wrecked the car and killed us both."

"Well, I didn't!" she snapped. He was enraged, agitated and totally distracted. Taking full advantage of his state, she snatched the car key from the ignition.

Cole's jaw dropped. He hadn't yet recovered from her shenanigans on the highway and now this! "Give me that key!" he demanded hoarsely.

"No! Now unlock the door and let me out. If you don't, I—I'll swallow the key. I swear I will."

He wouldn't put anything past her at this point. Cole took an immaculate white handkerchief from his pocket and wiped his brow. "You're behaving like a raving lunatic!"

"I'd rather be a raving lunatic than a weak-minded fool who meekly suffers your insults and then gets handed over to Seth Strickland." Chelsea slid across the seat, as far from him as she could get, clutching the car key in her fist.

"Chelsea, I am not going to hand you over to Strickland."

"You're damn right you aren't! I'm in charge of my own life. I spent my childhood and adolescence being bounced like a Ping-Pong ball between my parents and I've had it with other people using me to settle old scores! I'm not going to spend the rest of my life in that hapless role."

She stopped to catch her breath. Her voice was shaky as she spoke. "I was awake all last night, facing some painful truths about myself. Like why I happened to get involved with you and with Seth, two men who took over and assigned me to the sidelines of my own life. Like how I've subconsciously recreated situations similar to my powerless childhood as an adult with the men in my life."

It was an appalling revelation, but she'd taken enough psychology courses and read enough self-help books, to recognize a pattern of behavior and analyze its origins.

Her dark eyes blazed. "Maybe I had to reexperience those old feelings of helplessness to finally master them. But at last I have! Today proved it!"

Cole heaved an exasperated groan. "Kindly spare me the psychobabble." Unlike her, he'd always assiduously avoided psychology courses and self-help books. "Maybe the readers of your trendy little magazine find fascination and thrills in introspection and insights, but I don't."

"Naturally not. The all-powerful Cole Tremaine is too controlling and too repressed to risk acknowledging any potential weakness."

"Why does armchair analysis always end in character assassination?" muttered Cole. "Mine."

He scowled, his expression, his tone, disgruntled and aggrieved. Suddenly he seemed less the all-powerful and maddeningly self-possessed Cole Tremaine and more a cranky curmudgeon. Her lips twitched with unexpected amusement. "It doesn't always have to be negative, Cole. Analyzing encompasses positive attributes, too."

"But listing a person's positive attributes isn't any fun," he mocked. "Besides, you don't believe I have any."

She glanced at him, startled. Did he actually think that? "That's not true," she blurted out. "I know you have many good qualities."

"Then name two," he challenged.

"I can name a lot more than two." She didn't know why it was so important to assure him that she held his character in high regard. "You have a fine sense of humor. You're strong and dependable, loyal and hardworking. You're generous and thoughtful and," she paused, "considerate."

Both in and out of bed. The renegade thought leaped to mind, evoking all sorts of images and memories of the two of them together. She swallowed hard.

"Is that enough or shall I go on?" she asked lightly, feeling a warm blush of color stain her cheeks. Thank heavens he knew nothing of the wanton thoughts tripping through her brain.

"You don't have to lay it on any thicker," he said dryly. "Just refrain from comparing me to that preening pretty boy Strickland. We're nothing alike."

"Except you both made me feel passive and helpless, as if I had no control over my life." She sighed, her expression troubled. "Exactly the way I felt while I was growing up and my parents were fighting over Stefanie and me, dragging us into court for custody fights over and over again. Taking turns kidnapping us when the other had custody."

He started with surprise. "Your parents kidnapped you and Stefanie from each other?"

"Several times, back and forth. The method was always the same. Do you know how terrifying it is to be walking home from school only to be suddenly snatched off the streets and tossed into a car that speeds away? Of course you don't, but I do, only too well."

"You never told me any of that before," he said slowly. "You rarely mentioned your parents when we were together." Guilt crept through him. He'd snatched her off the road and into the car and sped away, evoking all those old childhood demons.

Chelsea stared at the floor. "Back then I didn't want to spend my time with you talking about divorce and hostility and rehashing bad memories. When I was with you I wanted to be charming and entertaining and—"

"Chelsea, I didn't expect you to be a source of perpetual entertainment. For God's sake, I wanted to marry you! You should've told me anything that would've helped me to understand you."

She shrugged. "I've always found my parents' vindictive craziness hard to talk about. Besides, we never delved into each other's minds or our pasts when we were together. We were too engrossed in the present."

"Doing things, going places, having fun, making love." Cole stared at her thoughtfully. "Everything couples do in a new relationship. If we'd had more time—"

"To get to know each other on a deeper level?" Chelsea interrupted softly. "You said we didn't need more time, remember? You wanted to get married immediately and when I refused *because we didn't know each other well enough*, you broke it off permanently between us."

Cole grimaced. She'd made her point and succinctly won the four-year-old argument hands down. It was one of the few times in his life he was bereft of speech.

Chelsea allowed herself to smile. Nobody knew better than she how much Cole hated to be bested. She felt herself soften toward him a little because she had done just that. "Cole, I want to apologize for grabbing the wheel. It *was* a crazy stunt, but there was something about being kidnapped again that made me just lose control."

"So I noticed. But it wasn't being kidnapped that freaked you out, Chelsea. You were dealing with that. You didn't turn into a frenzied maniac until I mentioned sex." He laughed wickedly. "Now *there's* a subject worthy of analysis. Why would the mere mention of sex drive an escapee from the First Wedding into a maniacal frenzy?"

Three

Her nostalgic feelings for him abruptly vanished. He was back to being her adversary again. "Stop it, Cole," she warned.

"Why should you object to being told that you loved getting laid?" he asked with maddening ingenuousness. "We both know it's the truth."

"Shut up, Cole!"

"Refuse to listen to the facts, hmm? Can it be that you loved getting laid by me but not Strickland?" He laughed when he heard her sharp intake of breath. "Aha! Has the armchair analyst zeroed in on the crux of the problem?"

She had heard the term "goaded beyond endurance"; she'd even used those words a time or two. But she'd never experienced that feeling physically until this moment when indignation and fury and some other fierce emotion that she couldn't put a name to joined forces within her, driving her to action.

She swung back her arm, blindly determined to slap that intolerable smile from his face. Her fist opened and the key fell to the floor. Neither she nor Cole noticed.

A split second before her hand could connect with his cheek, Cole caught her wrist in midair and jerked her toward him. Thrown completely off balance, Chelsea crashed into him. He bore the impact of her weight easily, holding her wrist with one hand, his other hand fastening on the curve of her hip.

Down they went, entwined together, sinking onto the thick, cushioned seat. It all happened so fast that Chelsea barely had time to register that her actions had gone awry. The fiery temper that had so often wreaked havoc on her determination to stay cool and calm had triumphed yet again. And landed her in trouble—big trouble—yet again.

"Well, well." Cole's voice was husky and deep. "Just like old times."

Chelsea perceived an edge of mockery in his tone and reacted at once. Fighting the insidious syrupy warmth flowing through her, she tried to pull away from him. Like a choke chain, the harder she pulled the tighter his grasp grew. She jerked her chin up to glare at him and saw only herself reflected in his mirrored sunglasses.

Her hand reached up to remove them. Their eyes met and clung for one long moment. His dark blue gaze was hot and rampantly sexual, and she felt a helpless, responsive tremulousness creep into her limbs—just like old times.

Chelsea's heart jumped and she felt abruptly breathless as his nearness unleashed a flood of disturbing sensual memories. The years seemed to roll away, catapulting her back into that place in time when she'd been deeply in love with Cole. How she'd needed him. How she'd wanted him.

Her body began to throb in aching reminiscence. She had always been powerfully attracted to him. Fireworks had gone off in her head the moment she'd met him. And now, despite their four-year separation, despite their bitter breakup, the chemistry still arced between them, as hot and compelling as before.

Cole drew her inexorably closer, until the heat emanating from his body burned into hers, kindling a fire in her belly that swiftly spread to every part of her. Chelsea was excruciatingly aware of her breasts crushed against the muscular wall of his chest, of the tingling in her nipples as they grew taut and sensitized. She felt a shocking urge to rub them against him, to soothe the sensual ache, to increase it. Their limbs were entangled intimately, his hard muscled thigh pressed high between her legs.

Their gazes held and she silently watched his head descend toward her. When his mouth hovered a half inch above her own, her eyelids closed of their own volition. Chelsea forced them open again and struggled to keep them open as Cole touched his lips to hers.

"Don't." She barely recognized the breathless, thready whisper as her own voice.

"You know you want me to." He flicked the tip of his tongue over her lips, teasing them apart. Releasing her wrist, he slid his palm along the length of her spine, lingering to massage the sensitive spot at the small of her back. Though she fought against it, Chelsea was unable to suppress the moan that shuddered through her.

"You're hungry, aren't you, baby?" Cole's mouth was hot and urgent on the sensitive curve of her neck. "It seems I can still make you want me after all this time." Just as he still wanted her.

Chelsea felt the unmistakable evidence of his desire as his hand slid from her hip to her bottom to position her even more intimately against him. Her senses rioted. Her mind was a battleground where common sense—urging her to put a stop to this at once—warred with years of pent-up yearning for just this moment.

"Cole, please, I—" Her voice faded into a soft gasp as he opened his mouth over hers to claim it with bold mastery. She felt his tongue thrust into her mouth and rub seductively against her tongue as it probed the moist, warm softness within.

She'd never been able to resist his kisses, and she responded like an addict to a drug. Her mind spun as her arms crept around his neck. She arched against him and began to move mindlessly, sinuously, feeling him thick and hard against the cradle of her femininity.

Inside the luxurious limousine with its darkened windows and plush upholstery, it was as if they were secluded in their own private zone, away and apart from everything and everyone. Cars and trucks whizzed by them on the highway, but Chelsea was oblivious to them; even the emotional upheavals of the day faded from her consciousness. Her world had narrowed to Cole and the sensations he was evoking within her.

She whimpered when his big hand slipped under the hem of her shirt to caress her bare back. There had been so many nights when she'd lain awake for hours, tossing and turning, her body feverish with a hunger that only Cole could assuage. And here they were, together again. For now, it seemed enough. Chelsea clung to him, kissing him with all of the passion within her.

"You're acting as if you missed me, Chelsea," he growled, keeping his lips lightly against hers. She made a small, unintelligible sound that didn't satisfy him. "Have you?" he demanded, kissing her deeply again and again. "Have you?"

"Yes," she admitted and moaned softly. She couldn't help it. Under her shirt, his hand was making a provocative foray toward her breasts.

"And Strickland?" he rasped. Just the thought of Seth Strickland touching Chelsea like this, kissing her, making love to her, burned him with scalding sexual jealousy. "Will you miss the way he made you feel?"

"No. No!" She was wound so tightly that it hurt to breathe. "We never made love. I didn't want to and he never pressed the issue." Sharing such intimacies with another man was unthinkable. "You're my first and only lover, Cole," she confessed dizzily.

Possessive sensuality burned in the dark blue depths of his eyes. "Good," he said fiercely. And then his thumb found the tight peak of her nipple, which was firm and pronounced beneath the soft silky material of her bra, and she found it impossible to think at all.

He pressed her nipple with the pad of his thumb and rubbed gently. She jerked spasmodically as desire, sharp and hot, sliced through her.

"You always were incredibly sensitive there," he whispered.

The low, gruff sound of his voice made her shiver with excitement. She well remembered that the more aroused he became, the deeper and rougher his tone.

He circled her nipple through the cloth, slowly, lazily, making it throb with a heat she felt deep inside her womb. She cried his name, her hands gripping his shoulders for support, as delicious tremors chased through her.

Her uninhibited response unleashed a passion within him that electrified as it astonished. After four years she still aroused him faster and harder than any other woman. The realization tripped off an alarm in his feverish brain. There had been a time when he'd been out of his head over her. She'd been his obsession, holding a power over him that no one ever had, before or since.

Just the thought of those dark days without her after their breakup had a jolting, sobering effect upon him. He had loved her and she'd broken his heart. It had taken a long,

long time for him to get over her and he'd vowed that no other woman would ever drag him under again.

And in the past four years, no other woman had even come close to penetrating his protective wall of reserve, to making him let go and lose control. But here was Chelsea, once again, threatening to do just that.

No, he promised himself, beating a strategic emotional withdrawal. Never again. Suddenly, the need to create distance between them was as vital as breathing.

"Hot, sexy little Chelsea." Cole drew back and laughed softly. "I bet I could get you to say anything right now. You've already admitted that there was nothing physical between you and Strickland, that you've never had any other man but me, that you've been missing me. I wonder what else you'd be willing to say and do?"

His light, biting tone penetrated the cocoon of sensuality enshrouding her. Chelsea opened her eyes slowly and gazed up at him. The expression on his face did not reassure her.

"All I have to do is to press the right buttons. Right, Chelsea? And I know exactly what and where they are, don't I, darling?" He sat up, taking her with him, then releasing her from his arms.

Chelsea returned to earth with a heart-shattering thud. She felt exposed and vulnerable and a sickening sense of dread was fast sweeping through her. "Is that why you kissed me? To prove that you could make me say and do—things?" She swallowed hard. "To humiliate me?"

"What do you think?" His blue eyes were glittering. "That I did it because I'm still in love with you?"

The confusion on her face and the pain that instantly shadowed her dark eyes almost made him apologize for his cruelty. Just as quickly, he talked himself out of that intention. He hadn't meant to touch her, but once he had, it had been impossible not to give reign to the explosive feelings she evoked. With Chelsea in his arms, he'd come dangerously near to forgetting his vow never to let her work him over again. The realization that she retained such power over him came as a profound shock. Fighting back was a necessity.

"I know you're not still in love with me." Chelsea slid across the seat, away from him, striving to regain her lost control. It wasn't easy; she was bewildered and hurt and angry all at once. Completely off balance. *Exactly the way Cole had boasted that he made women feel in his new heartbreaker persona.* He'd done this to her deliberately for his own amusement, using her, baiting her while she...

It was too much. She erupted with rage. "I don't think you ever loved me, not really. You loved the idea of having a compliant, mindless little wife and breeder! I was supposed to marry you on the date you set, I was supposed to have six children, two years apart because you liked the idea of a big family, and I wasn't allowed to offer an opinion concerning any of it."

"That's not true!" He shot back and yet, and yet...

Her words breached his defenses and he recognized a kernel of truth in them. Hadn't he laid out their future according to *his* plans, assuming that she would gladly go along? Hadn't he believed that she would want exactly what he did, because they were in love? That he might share the blame for what had gone wrong between them was a revolutionary concept. And not one he cared to contemplate at the moment, not after all these years of seeing himself as the innocent, wronged party.

But while Cole was caught up in thought, Chelsea was all action. She made a dive across the seat and grabbed the car key from the floor where it had been laying unnoticed.

"I'm going to drive back and get my car," she announced boldly, holding up the key in triumph. "If you want to come along for the ride, fine. If not, get out now."

Cole laughed. He couldn't help it. The idea of her commandeering his car was ludicrous. With his superior size and strength, he could easily overpower her; if he wanted, he could get the key back in a few seconds flat. It was incredibly tempting to contemplate. First he would grab her arms and wrestle her down onto the seat, then he would use his legs to pin her there, beneath him. She would struggle, of course, but he would have her on her back . . .

His eyes glazed as the scenario enfolded in his mind. He would be on top of her, pressing down on every soft inch of her body. Her breasts, her belly, her thighs would be grinding into his as she struggled to get free. His breathing grew labored as if he were already involved in that erotic tussle.

Erotic. He swallowed. Therein lay the trap. He might as well not kid himself, if he were lying on top of Chelsea, if she were moving beneath him, it would take all of one minute—if that long—before he covered her mouth with his. And once his tongue was in her mouth, his hands would naturally seek her breasts. Her struggles would cease as the kiss deepened. She would sigh and arch beneath him . . .

His mouth grew dry and his body began to throb, growing even harder than he already was. He was still aroused from their previous scuffle, which had swiftly escalated into passion. If he were to touch her again, it would happen even faster. She had that effect on him, she always had.

Which was why he could not—he would not!—succumb to her spell again. He had worked so hard to get her out of his system, he wouldn't allow himself to be sexually bewitched by her again.

"If you unlock the door, I'll get out and ride in the back," he said, abruptly straightening in his seat. "You can play chauffeur."

Chelsea's eyes met his and the hardness in those icy blue depths chilled her. He told her how to release the power lock and she followed his instructions warily, wondering if there was some catch in his sudden cooperation.

But Cole did as he said, leaving her alone in the front to climb into the roomy interior of the limousine and settle back on the long, wide seat. "Keep in mind that I'm letting you go because I want to," he said coolly, helping himself to a drink from the well-stocked bar there. "Just as I'm letting you drive because it suits me. If I'd felt like keeping you with me, there would be nothing you could do to make me let you go."

If he'd meant to completely squash whatever thrill her small victory had brought, he succeeded. Ridiculous as she knew it was, Chelsea actually felt rejected. Crossly, she started the car. She was not going to fall victim to Cole's manipulative mind-games, she lectured herself sternly. She had won her freedom and she ought to be glorying in her own cleverness and strength.

"I'm going to put on the radio," she announced, trying to sound like the victor in this fight. She assured herself that she even felt brave enough to cope with hearing the official cancellation of her wedding.

"Suit yourself. I have some calls to make," Cole replied impassively, picking up the cellular phone.

Chelsea was pulling onto the highway when she heard Cole's voice, deep and warm, resounding from the back of the limo. "Hello, Carling..."

Her heart sank like a stone. Jealousy, as corrosive as acid, made her want to scream with pain. But she didn't make a sound. Keeping her quivering lips pressed tightly together, she touched the small button with the pictograph of a window on it and a long partition of glass, separating the front from the back slid into place.

Fighting tears, she kept on driving to the nearest exit. She was furious with herself for her stupid, useless jealousy and furious with Cole for having the power to evoke it.

And she was so confused. After allowing herself to be railroaded into the First Wedding mania by the Stricklands, she thought she had finally gotten her life back on track this morning. Then Cole had appeared and she'd been seriously derailed once more.

It was devastating to realize how much she still wanted him, that he could still hurt her badly enough to make her cry. But then, deep in her heart, hadn't she known that all along?

Chelsea made herself face the uncomfortable truth. If she hadn't heard those rumors of Cole's involvement with Carling Templeton, she never would have dated Seth Strickland in the first place. She'd let herself be used by Seth and the Stricklands in their gigantic public relations campaign, but she had used them, too, she acknowledged with silent regret. As a defense against the pain she was suffering at the thought of Cole in love with the beautiful, sophisticated Carling.

Carling and Cole. Her heart clenched. She hadn't given the other woman a thought when Cole had taken her in his arms. He hadn't forgotten Seth Strickland, though. He'd brought up the other man's name and smiled with satisfaction when she'd completely repudiated him. Though she'd been too far gone at the time to be mortified by her abject surrender, she cringed now, retrospectively. Had it all been part of Cole's revenge? To make her admit she wanted him even though he was out of reach, involved with another woman?

A flash of blazing anger seared her. The man was a manipulative, coldhearted snake!

The route back to her car was long and circuitous. She had to get off the interstate at the next exit, then get back on, heading in the opposite direction. Then, off at the exit beyond where she'd parked, and back on again in the westbound lanes.

But Chelsea hardly noticed the length and distance of the drive; there were too many other things competing for her attention. Every time she flicked a glance toward the back and saw Cole, smiling as he talked into the phone—*to Carling!*—her blood boiled.

And then the announcement she'd been both anticipating and dreading came over the airwaves. The White House wedding had been postponed temporarily due to the sudden, serious illness of Miss Chelsea Kincaid. That the devoted bridegroom-to-be was allegedly at his beloved's side in some undisclosed hospital.

Chelsea was horrified at the blatant lie. And gripped by icy terror. What did it mean? Why would they release such a statement? Seth's threats echoed in her head. *You're going to marry me whether you want to or not. I'll force you if I have to, I'll do whatever it takes to make you go through with this damn wedding.*

Her imagination ran wild, visualizing all kinds of frightening possibilities. The Stricklands could hire a gang of thugs to go after her and beat her up, then take her to that "undisclosed hospital" she was already supposed to be in. And once in their power, they could drug her with horrible drugs.

By the time she pulled the limousine behind her hobbled little Honda, Chelsea was sick with fear. The migraine she'd been trying to keep at bay arrived in full force, but the pain pounding in her head was dwarfed by the panic surging through her. She wanted to beg Cole to help her, but she didn't dare. He'd changed his mind about returning her to Seth once and she didn't dare risk him changing it back again.

No, she had to face this on her own. Alone. She climbed from the limousine, her head aching, her eyes watering from the brightness of the sun, gulping back the nausea raging through her. She had never felt so alone or so desolate in her entire life.

Cole resumed his rightful place behind the wheel. He stared hard at her through narrowed eyes. "You don't look very well," he observed, frowning.

"I'm fine," she insisted. Deep in her heart, she couldn't believe that he was enemy enough to turn her over to the Stricklands, but she was too distraught to trust her own instincts. It wasn't as if she could stay with Cole anyway, even if he were to offer, not with Carling in the picture. The prospect of holing up somewhere with him and the senator's lovely daughter was enough to make her gag.

"Are you sure you don't want to come with me?" he asked in a suggestive, insulting tone, guaranteed to enrage any discerning woman. His dark blue eyes were as cold as ice.

Chelsea, a discerning woman, was suitably enraged. "No, I don't want to come with you. I'm in charge of my own life, remember? And that means making my own choices and not submissively ceding control to you. I'm going to change the tire and leave in my own car."

He gave a disparaging laugh. "You couldn't change a tire if your life depended on it."

"Of course a snake like you would never bother to change the tire for me." She couldn't help hoping that he'd take her up on her derisive challenge and do it.

He didn't. "That's right. We snakes eat nasty little shrews like you for lunch, we don't do them any favors."

"I wouldn't let you do me a favor. Not even if you got down on your knees and begged me!"

"I seem to recall a time when I was on my knees in front of you. About four years ago, in my bedroom." He flashed a reckless, insolent smile, his blue eyes hard and piercing. "You were lying naked on the edge of my bed and you were the one who was begging."

Her heart stopped, then started with a violent lurch as the images he'd evoked played before her mind's eye, complete with sound effects. For a moment she was immobilized by the force of it.

"I hate you," she gritted out, fighting to pull herself back together. She felt so vulnerable and shaken with rage. How dare he call back such intimate moments and use them as weapons against her? "You're an unspeakable bastard."

He merely raised his eyebrows. "What upsets you the most, Chelsea? That I dared to mention such an episode from our torrid past? Or that you wish you were back on that bed, moaning for me to—"

"Get out of here and leave me alone!" Seething, blushing, trembling, she rushed away from the limousine to her own car, pausing to call over her shoulder, "I never want to see you again. With any luck, I'll never have to!"

"Be careful what you wish for, darling," he taunted through the open window, "because you just might get it. Like now, for instance. I am out of here and out of your life."

With a feral grin and a jaunty honk of the horn, he pulled the limousine back into the stream of highway traffic. He permitted himself just one glance at Chelsea through the rearview mirror. She was fumbling with the keys to the trunk of her car, not even looking in his direction.

Or so he thought. Her head averted, from the corner of her eye, Chelsea watched the limo until it rounded the bend and disappeared from view. So he'd left her. She decided it was a good thing she was so infuriated or she would have burst into tears.

Her head hurt so badly that she decided to take two of her headache pills before attempting to tangle with the tire. And then it struck her. Her suitcase—with her clothes, medicine, cosmetics, credit cards and most of her money—was still in Cole's car! She had a small purse with a few basic essentials like her driver's license, comb and lipstick. She had a few dollars tucked in the front seat of her car. But everything else she'd packed in her suitcase, which had just gone speeding off with Cole.

She didn't know whether to cry or to curse. So she did a little of both. What was she going to do now? Chelsea retrieved her purse and peered inside it, as if willing her medication and money to somehow miraculously appear. Of course, it didn't happen.

Her only hope was to change the tire, drive to the nearest exit, find a phone and call Stefanie for help. Hopefully, her younger sister would make the two-hour trip to her side and deliver a fresh supply of migraine pills, clothes and other necessities she would need while in hiding. Chelsea gnawed her lower lip, thinking back to her last phone call to Stefanie early this morning, right after she'd called Seth to cancel the wedding.

"The wedding's off and I'm leaving town," she said quickly, not giving her sister time to interject a single world. "I want you to tell Mother and Dad."

Stefanie's shriek of horror had reverberated in her eardrum. Chelsea understood her sister's reaction perfectly. Having to tell Janice Jarvis Kincaid Emerson and Ross Kincaid about the aborted wedding was definitely something to scream about. Her parents had flipped when she'd broken her engagement to Cole, then they'd launched into a mega-brouhaha of accusations and counteraccusations, each blaming the other for their daughter's behavior. Their response to the news of the canceled wedding would probably register on the Richter scale.

And poor Stefanie would have to be there for it. Maybe she'd welcome the two-hour emergency trip as a bit of well-deserved R and R. Chelsea straightened her shoulders and tried to rally her spirits. The sooner she changed the tire, the sooner this nightmare—and this migraine!—would be over.

"You couldn't change a tire if your life depended on it." Cole's jeer rang in her ears. Well, her life did depend on it, sort of.

"I can do it," she said aloud.

She removed the jack from the trunk of her car and stared at it triumphantly. Cole Tremaine probably thought she didn't even know one needed a jack to change a tire. Well, she did know and she had it and she was going to change the stupid tire!

Four

She was studying the configuration of jack and tire, wondering how they fit together, when a beat-up green Chevy pulled onto the shoulder of the road, several yards behind her car. Two men, one tall and rather good-looking in a scruffy sort of way, the other short and boyish with glasses, both wearing chinos and sports shirts, climbed out.

Chelsea stood up, apprehension gnawing at her. She could always hope that they'd stopped to help a motorist in distress. If they happened to have other ideas concerning a vulnerable woman alone... Her fingers tightened around the jack. It was a formidable weapon, she told herself bracingly.

"Hi!" she called, sounding far more confident than she felt. She forced herself to smile. Hadn't the self-defense book she'd read claimed that if one acted like a potential victim, one might end up being exactly that? "My tire seems to have gone flat and I'm going to change it." She shifted the jack from one hand to another.

The short man gaped at her. "Hell's bells!" he exclaimed excitedly. "It's really you—Chelsea Kincaid!"

Chelsea suppressed a groan. It was too much to hope that she wouldn't be recognized. "That's right," she admitted, for what was the use in denying it. "Who are you?"

"We're the press," the short man said eagerly, whipping out a tattered card, presumably his press credentials, from his pants pocket. "I'm Miles Rodgers, a photographer with *Globe Star Probe*. And he is Kieran Kaufman, one of our top reporters."

"The *Globe Star Probe*!" Chelsea recoiled with disgust. "That's not the press, that's toxic waste! That sleazy rag makes all the other tabloids look like the *Wall Street Journal*."

"Thanks, I think." Miles Rodgers beamed.

Chelsea regarded him sternly. "The *Globe Star Probe* is nothing but sensationalistic trash with no redeeming qualities whatsoever." She was too offended to be cautious or diplomatic. "It's the lowest of the low. I wouldn't even use it to line a bird cage, if I had a bird."

"It's true we at the *Probe* don't get a lot of respect. In fact we don't get any, that's why we have to try harder," Kieran Kaufman said genially. "But we're beating all the big shots with this scoop. You see, Miss Kincaid—Chelsea, if I may—we're the first to find you, and you're not in the hospital like the Prez said. You don't even look sick to me."

Chelsea thought of the official White House announcement and her stomach lurched. The pain in her head intensified as she rubbed her forehead with her fingertips. Even the skin hurt to touch. "Well, you're wrong. I have a killer migraine. I have to change a tire, and now you two are here to concoct one of the *Probe*'s sleazy prevarications. I feel sick, all right."

"Migraine, huh? Maybe I can help. I wrote about migraines once for the *Probe*'s health column." Kaufman grinned. "According to my research, one-quarter of the migraine sufferers polled reported that orgasm helped soothe the pain, and the stronger the orgasm, the greater the relief. So if you'd care to climb in the backseat of the car with me, I'll be happy to—"

"You slime!" Chelsea interrupted, incensed. She raised the jack threateningly. "Get away from me. I don't want to talk to you and I most definitely don't want to *listen* to you."

Kaufman shrugged. "I swiped the article from *New Age Holistic Health*, babe. It's legit. But if you'd rather go on suffering, it's your headache. Miles and I are here to find out the real reason why the First Wedding turned into the Big Dump."

"How did you find me?" Chelsea demanded. And who else was on her trail? she wondered.

"We have our sources," Miles said proudly. "One of Kieran's sweeties is a receptionist who works at a certain—shall we say, clandestine?—private detective agency. She couldn't believe it when a confidential call came in to track down Chelsea Kincaid, and on the very morning of the big wedding, too. She called Kier right away."

"So much for confidential calls," said Chelsea, rolling her eyes. "What did the agency do?"

"Sent out three investigators in cheap suits in a big black Lincoln to go after the lost bride and bring her back," replied Kieran Kaufman. "Wonder if Strickland meant dead or alive?" he added, chuckling at his own joke.

Chelsea didn't crack a smile. She glowered fiercely at them.

"We've been monitoring their calls on our CB," continued Kaufman. "We know they're heading west on I-70, so we raced ahead of them. We wanted to find you before they did."

He and Miles Rodgers slapped their palms together in self-congratulatory high-fives. "Kieran, my friend, this is the story that will put us back in the newsroom!" exulted Miles. "We'll be doing *real* news again! We'll be able to write our ticket to any paper or station in the country. Uh, excluding Channel Five, that is."

"Channel Five? In Washington?" Chelsea stared, a light dawning. "You're *that* Kieran Kaufman? The reporter Channel Five fired after you accidentally substituted your own private X-rated videotape for what was supposed to be a taped interview with a visiting Olympic gymnast? It aired on the six p.m. newscast, the one with the highest number of children and senior citizens viewing."

"Bad career move," Kaufman admitted. "Nobody cared that it was an accident and the station manager and network chiefs went crazy. I was blackballed by everyone, everywhere, except the *Globe Star Probe*. I've been trying to get back into legitimate news ever since. Miles has, too. A few years back, he was Channel Five's weekend anchorman with a bit of a drinking problem. An unfortunate combination."

"I showed up drunk for the broadcast and passed out on the air during the Saturday News at Eleven," Miles affirmed ruefully. "I was fired on the spot."

"But he's beaten that and is ready to hit the big time," interjected Kieran. "This story will establish us as professional newsmen again! You're coming with us, angel face. You're going to give us the exclusive story of why you ran out on Seth Strickland. We have video equipment set up in my apartment and Miles and I will take turns interviewing you on tape. And then—" he paused and sighed, his expression rapturous "—we'll sell the tape to the highest bidder. And not only will we demand top price for it, we'll also demand TV reporting jobs."

"I'm not going anywhere with you," Chelsea said defiantly, backing away from them, clutching the jack with trembling fingers.

Kieran Kaufman's smile abruptly vanished. "Oh yeah you are, princess. And you'll talk." He didn't add the inevitable "or else," but the implied threat was unmistakable.

"Chelsea, sweetie, don't make this hard on yourself," coaxed Miles. "We don't want any trouble."

"And making Kieran Kaufman lose his temper is big trouble, babe," Kaufman informed her archly. "Now let's go quietly, okay?" He took a step toward her.

"Never. I'll make a scene," Chelsea warned. She was somewhere beyond fear now. The emotional toll of the day and the pain of her headache had catapulted her into a twilight zone of unreality. She felt almost detached from the scene, as if she were standing outside herself, watching someone else act the part of Chelsea Kincaid. "I'll scream and fight and someone will be sure to pull over and stop to help me. And then I'll press charges against you—terrorist threats and—and conspiracy and—"

"Yeah, yeah," Kaufman continued his advance. "People threaten us all the time, honey. We don't care. It's all in a day's work."

"Don't look so scared, Chelsea," Miles Rodgers said soothingly. "We're not going to hurt you. It's just that this story is our big chance and we have to take advantage of it."

"You mean take advantage of *me*!" Chelsea moved closer to the road. If only someone would stop! She looked at the speeding cars, at the enormous tractor-trailers that shook the ground as they roared by. None of them slowed down; their drivers evinced no interest whatsoever in the young woman stranded alongside the road.

"Try to put a positive spin on all this," Miles said encouragingly. "You'll get to tell your side of the split. Since Strickland has already lied about why the wedding was cancelled, his credibility will be zero. You can say whatever you want about him and people will believe you. You can really stick it to him."

"I don't want to stick it to him!" Chelsea exclaimed. "I just don't want to marry him, that's all."

"Ever seen him drunk?" Kieran pressed eagerly. "Ever seen him do coke? Any paternity suits the family has hushed up? What about peculiar sexual habits, you know, kinky stuff like cross-dressing or—"

"If you say another word, I'm going to hit you with this," Chelsea injected furiously, brandishing the jack like a sword. "I swear I will. And it'll hurt, too."

"The lady's tough." Kaufman laughed. "Aren't you scared, Miles?"

"I'm shivering with fear," Miles chortled. And then his smile faded as he squinted at the highway. "Uh-oh, look who's here. Damn, I thought they were farther behind us! It's those bozos from the agency that the Stricklands hired."

A black Lincoln screeched to a halt behind the reporters' car. Chelsea's eyes widened as three men in shiny, dark suits simultaneously jumped out of the car and hurried toward them.

Kieran Kaufman cursed. Miles Rodgers reached into his shirt pocket and pulled out a half-eaten roll of antacid tables, then popped two in his mouth.

"You were right about their suits, Kier," Miles observed. "They're so cheap they look like rejects from a bargain basement fire sale."

Chelsea was not interested in the quality of the men's suits. "Are they really detectives?" she whispered, her pulse resounding painfully in her head.

"Not reputable, licensed ones," Kaufman replied. "They'll do anything for a buck. The *Globe Star Probe* has used that agency on occasion. Need I say more?"

"You're Chelsea Kincaid!" one of the detectives informed her triumphantly.

"She knows who she is," retorted Miles Rodgers, scowling at the men.

"Stunning piece of detective work," Kaufman added disdainfully. "You guys are worth every penny Strickland pays you. You know, it blows me away that the illustrious Stricklands even know that your agency exists. They're supposedly so wholesome and high-minded and you guys have a known rep for operating outside the law whenever it suits you."

"We bend the laws when we have to," another of the detectives admitted with a shrug. He made a move toward Chelsea. "Be a good girl and come quietly, Miss Kincaid. Your husband-to-be can't wait to get his hands on you."

"Neither can we," snorted the third dark suit. "Let's go, sugar. We're taking you with us."

"No!" Chelsea, Kieran and Miles chorused together.

"We found her first," Miles said indignantly. "She's coming with us, aren't you, Chelsea?"

Chelsea swallowed. The three detectives were big men, tall and strong and ugly. They looked mean and threatening, just the sort who would beat a woman badly enough to land her in a hospital—and enjoy every minute of it. She shrank behind the two reporters, aware of the irony of her newfound alliance but not caring.

"Like hell she is. Who are you?" The biggest man in a dark suit demanded the identity of Kaufman and Rodgers.

"They're with the *Globe Star Probe*," replied Chelsea, inching slowly from behind her human shield. If she could make it to her car, she could lock herself in it and lay on the horn. She wouldn't let up until another driver stopped.

"They're going to write a front-page exclusive about my disappearance aboard a UFO. In a couple months they'll write a follow-up about me giving birth to an alien's baby, complete with exclusive photographs."

Miles Rodgers chuckled. Kieran Kaufman groaned. The other three men sneered, their expressions definitely threatening. "We've wasted enough time," said the detective whose bulk made a studio wrestler look petite. "Grab her and let's go."

"You can't have her," snapped Kaufman. "She's ours."

"I'm not going with any of you." Chelsea, her purse tucked under one arm, held the jack in front of her like a shield. "You don't scare me," she said, wishing it were true, wishing that her voice wouldn't shake so, that her knees didn't feel ready to buckle. "Don't come any nearer, I'm warning you."

All five men laughed at that. And while they were laughing and Chelsea was wondering what on earth she was going to do when they stopped and came after her, a car—another enormous, black stretch limousine—seemed to appear out of nowhere and grind to a halt beside her.

The front passenger door was flung open. "Chelsea, get in!" ordered Cole.

She didn't have to be told twice. Dropping the jack, she jumped in, pulling the door closed as Cole peeled off the shoulder and back onto the road. He took off at a ferocious rate of speed, leaving the others in his dust.

"Oh, Cole, I was so scared!" Chelsea whispered, leaning her head against the cushioned head rest. She closed her eyes and tears of relief, of delayed terror, burned her behind her lids. Her head felt as if an interior anvil was smashing against the inside of her skull.

"What was going on back there?" Cole demanded, veering into the passing lane and fairly flying past the rest of the traffic. "Who were those men and what were they doing there?"

"Two of them were reporters from the *Globe Star Probe*." She had to gulp back a sob. It was hard to talk around the huge lump lodged in her throat.

Cole groaned with disgust.

"They were knights in shining armor compared to the three so-called detectives from some shady agency that the Stricklands hired to find me." Chelsea shuddered. "If you hadn't come when you did..." She lost her battle to keep the tears at bay and they spilled down her cheeks.

"Did they hurt you, Chelsea?" Cole asked tautly.

"No." She shook her head and the movement caused a piercingly sharp pain that made her wince. With shaking fingers, she opened her small purse, pulled out a tissue and rubbed her tears away. "They scared me, that's all. And I'm still scared. I don't know what I'm going to do or where I'm going to go. They'll follow us, I know, and if they find me... I'll probably *need* to be hospitalized after those thugs are through with me, and Kaufman and Rodgers have big plans for a videotape of me accusing Seth of depravity and—and—" Her voice trailed off and she choked back another sob.

"They're not going to find you. We have a substantial lead on them, even if they do try to follow. You must try to calm down, Chelsea."

"I can't!" she wailed. "This has been one of the worst days of my life. Every time I turn around someone shows up planning to kidnap me. I'm probably going to have to spend the rest of my years as a fugitive on the run and—and my head hurts so much it feels like a bomb is exploding in it."

"I'm not surprised you have a migraine," Cole said wryly. "As you said, this hasn't been one of your better days. Do you have your pain pills with you?"

"In my suitcase. Which you drove off with," she added with a touch of asperity.

His lips curved into a sardonic smile. "You ordered me to leave, remember? Said you never wanted to see me again." He laughed dryly. "You certainly changed your mind in a hurry. You couldn't get in the car fast enough."

"I decided better the devil you know than the Gang of Five back there," Chelsea retorted with a flash of spirit. "Cole," she turned slowly to gaze at him with wide brown eyes. "Earlier you said that you were kidnapping me for revenge."

"I believe I did say something along those lines," he agreed glibly.

"Cole, if you're secretly in cahoots with the Stricklands, please tell me now."

"Why? So you can make another grab for the steering wheel?"

She did not return his grin, but continued to stare at him anxiously.

Cole sighed. "I am not now, nor ever will be 'in cahoots' with the Stricklands, secretly or otherwise, Chelsea. Now climb into the back and get your pain pills."

She did so, rummaging through her suitcase until she came up with the vial of pills prescribed for migraine pain.

"You'll need some liquid to take the pills," said Cole, covertly watching her through the rearview mirror. "Get something to drink from the bar. No alcohol, either a soft drink without caffeine or some fruit juice. And then lie down back there. Stretch out on the seat and close your eyes."

There were times when his take-over-and-give-orders executive air drove her crazy. Not this time. She was too grateful for his presence, for his help and concern. She downed two of the pills with swallows of canned juice.

Then, because her head was killing her, she gulped down two more, in the hope that a double dose would work faster.

The moment after she'd swallowed them, she acknowledged that taking four pills instead of two was one more stupid action to add to the ever-growing list of reckless, risky things she'd done lately. She was disgusted with herself. Lucky for her the dosage was too low to have any toxic effects but she promised herself that from now on she would think before she gulped down anything!

The upholstery was deep and soft as down-filled pillows, but she was unable to relax and appreciate the comfort. Her muscles were still taut with tension, her nerves wound tightly on edge. Worst of all, her headache hadn't improved one iota.

She sat back up. "Cole, what if—"

"Lie down and be quiet," he commanded.

"It's no use, the pills aren't working. I—"

"Give them a little time. You've barely swallowed them. Now close your eyes and go to sleep. That's the only thing that'll cure your headache."

"I can't, it feels like there's a volcano erupting inside my head. I'm too wired to sleep anyway. My car is abandoned on the road and you still haven't told me where you're taking me and why."

"I'll call and arrange for your car to be returned to the parking lot of your apartment building. As for the other...let's just say I have my own agenda."

Cole gave a short, self-mocking laugh. And if he could figure out what it was, he might also learn why he was zooming up and down the interstate like a trolling maniac. His behavior today had been completely out of character: spontaneous, irrational and totally inexcusable.

It was bad enough that he'd followed Chelsea from the city, that he had forced her into his car the first time and driven off with her like some kind of marauding pirate. He had to compound those errors by kissing her; his body was still hard and throbbing from that impetuous lapse.

Still, he had come to his senses in time to let her go. When he'd permitted her to drive herself back to her car, he had fully intended to change her tire and send her on her way. Unfortunately, he had somehow wavered from that noble course. He didn't bother to deny to himself that he had instigated their flaming fight—and he had driven off, leaving her alone and stranded on the highway.

He'd regretted his rash and totally unchivalrous action the moment he had pulled the limo into traffic. He was appalled with himself. This wasn't how a former Eagle Scout acted! He had always been the responsible, good-citizen type, holding doors for mothers carrying toddlers and packages, returning supermarket shopping carts to the front door of the building, stopping to help fellow motorists change flat tires when he saw them stranded alongside the road.

But he'd left Chelsea, alone and unprotected, and driven off in a fit of temper.

Since driving backward on an interstate highway was illegal and impossible, he had no choice but to drive to the next exit and then double back. And while he followed that tedious route, he alternately berated himself for behavior unbecoming a Tremaine and tormented himself with images of Chelsea meeting with some kind of unspeakable harm while in such vulnerable straits.

His heart had leaped into his throat at the sight of her standing perilously close to the edge of the road; then he'd noticed the five men. Of course there was a chance that they'd all stopped because their altruistic nature were inspired by the plight of a helpless young woman in need of assistance.

But his instincts told him otherwise. If everything was all right, Chelsea could tell him so as he idled his car alongside her. Instead, she'd jumped inside, her expression leaving no doubt that the faster they moved out, the better.

She was in trouble. Seth Strickland wanted her, his hired goons wanted her and the two slimy reporters wanted her. And he, Cole Tremaine, had her.

He permitted himself a swift glance at her in the rearview mirror. And almost groaned with despair. Would the day ever come when he could look at her and not feel his senses reel? Everything about her captivated him. Her skin, as soft and white as the petals of a camellia, flawless except for the smattering of pale freckles across her nose, a legacy of a long-ago sunburn that had defied sunblock. Her huge, expressive velvety-brown eyes that seemed to change with her emotions—going dark when she was angry, bright with laughter when she was amused and becoming soft and luminous when she was aroused with passion.

He watched her capture her lower lip between her teeth and felt the effects of the small gesture deep in his groin. Her mouth was indescribably sensual, her lips full and beautifully shaped, her teeth small and white.

And if he wanted to continue to torture himself, he could concentrate on the graceful, slender curve of her neck, or her compact but sweetly rounded breasts rising and falling beneath her cotton shirt, or her long, slim legs and how they'd felt wrapped around him when they'd made love.

Cole inhaled sharply. He was falling under her spell again and part of him wanted to let himself succumb to her charms and stop fighting his feelings. But a stronger, tougher side of him—the survivor who'd spent most of his childhood without maternal tenderness, the competitor who refused to quit until he'd won—rebelled at the prospect. He'd once given her his heart and his love—and look how *that* had turned out!

He'd been left holding the diamond ring he had bought her, along with drinks and dinner for two hundred. Cole's jaw tensed and his mouth went taut. No, he was not going to let her work him over, drag him under, or tie him in knots again.

He might still want her physically, but this time his emotions were not involved, he assured himself. A sudden wolfish grin crossed his face. She wanted him, too; her response to his kiss earlier today had proven that. A wholly unscrupulous idea sprang to mind. Why couldn't he have her sexually, without any of the sentiment and emotional entanglement that had proved his undoing the last time around with her?

Why couldn't they have an affair based strictly on physical passion? He cast another hungry glance at her. Why not indeed?

He could sexually sate himself with her without having the responsibility of caring for her, of caring about her. From the first time they'd made love, he had cherished her as the woman he wanted to marry, as the future mother of his children. This time, it would be strictly sex. Thrilling, mind-blowing, passion-quenching sex.

And this time he wouldn't get hurt. He'd know from the start that it was temporary and based solely on physical attraction. He wouldn't make the mistake of making a commitment or expecting one from her. And maybe, when it was over, he would finally get out of this holding pattern he'd been in for the past four years, unwilling and unable to seriously interest himself in another woman. After all, when he and Chelsea had broken up he'd still wanted her. How many of these residual feelings he had for her were because she was "the one who got away?"

There was just one major flaw in his plan. He knew very well that Chelsea would never consent to meaningless sex; she had to believe that she was in love...and that her love was returned. His lips curved into a cynical smile. Surely the new Cole Tremaine could pull that one off.

The Eagle Scout who still lived within him protested at once. He'd always been fair in his dealings with women, never making false promises, or permitting any delusions as to his intentions. If he'd gained a reputation as a smooth operator, he was at least an honest one, promising strictly a good time and never a commitment.

But he would be duping Chelsea as much as she would be duping herself, he insisted to himself. He would have to bait his trap carefully.

"You haven't told me your own agenda." Chelsea's voice roused him from his reverie. She was sitting up now, watching him, her big, brown eyes wary. He reminded her of a shark who'd just spotted a group of swimmers and was contemplating lunch. "Why did you come back for me, Cole? And where are you taking me?"

He smiled, a shark who'd decided that *she* was his lunch.

"I came back for you because my conscience wouldn't let me abandon a woman along the highway without helping her," Cole replied. Might as well keep the old Eagle Scout within him happy and tell the partial truth.

"And you do need my help, Chelsea. You're on the run from an assortment of unsavory types and you need a place to hide until the media storm blows over."

"I know I'm in trouble, but you may be too, Cole. Suppose one of those intrepid trackers took down your license-plate number when you stopped for me? They'll be able to trace this car to Tremaine Incorporated. And it's no big secret that we were once engaged. If they suspect you of helping me, you'll be in danger, too!"

"I'm not afraid of the Stricklands." Cole laughed at the very notion. "Sweetheart, I can personally buy and sell them five times over."

"But money can't protect you if they want revenge!"

"Of course it can, Chelsea. For starters, I can provide a place where you'll be completely out of reach of the Stricklands and their henchmen, as well as reporters. And a few well-placed phone calls from me will defuse any further threat from them."

The bait was in the trap.

Chelsea held her breath. Did she dare to hope? "You—you wouldn't mind helping me?" She approached the metaphorical bait with trepidation and a desperation that delighted him.

"My family has a cabin in the Catoctin Mountains in northwest Maryland. The place is so remote that it's impossible to find without exact knowledge of the location. But it's extremely comfortable, a real vacation home. And, of course, the security is first rate."

A Tremaine wouldn't settle for anything less, she knew. Her eyes widened. "You'd let me stay there?"

"Yes." He nodded, pleased. She was entering the trap. "Just for curiosity's sake, where had you planned to go when you left Washington?" he asked idly.

"I didn't have any real destination in mind. I planned to drive west until I got far enough away from the city or was too tired to drive anymore or whatever came first. I guess I thought I would get off the interstate and hole up in some nondescript little motel in rural Maryland or Pennsylvania or West Virginia. Wherever I happened to stop."

"You think that people in rural areas don't keep up with the news? Sorry to shatter your illusions, honey, but who do you think buys those gigantic satellite dishes enabling them to tune in six hundred TV stations from around the world? You'd have been recognized and found in a day, maybe less."

"I wasn't thinking too clearly after I talked to Seth, I just knew I had to get away. Cole, did you hear the official announcement? They said the wedding had been postponed because I was sick and in the hospital."

"And they sent the goon squad after you, so they obviously haven't given up the idea of the First Wedding, even an involuntary one." His lips thinned into a straight line. "Strickland is really hung up on you, isn't he?"

"Of course not! Seth doesn't love me. He's deeply and totally in love with himself. The only reason he wanted to get married in the first place was because he was disturbed by a snide article that a conservative columnist wrote about him, hinting that maybe something was wrong with the President's son because he was thirty-two years old and had never been married."

"I'm almost thirty-five and I've never been married," Cole protested, "and there's nothing *wrong* with me!" Had all gone according to his plans, he'd have been married four years ago and would already have a couple of kids. He directed a frown of disapproval at Chelsea.

Who didn't catch it. "But you're not the President's son," she continued earnestly. "So sly political columnists don't print innuendos about you. When I met Seth that night at the Bulgarian Embassy party—"

"Bulgarian Embassy, huh? Now there's a fairy-tale setting for a romance," Cole interjected tartly.

She grimaced, ignoring the jibe. "All Seth could talk about was that column. He was obsessed with it, and determined to find a bride. As soon as I started going out with him, the Strickland publicity machine began to roll."

"Your explanation is a little too self-serving for me, darling. You weren't the first woman Strickland ever dated, you know. He's handsome, rich, well-connected. He has a reputation as a rake, in fact he goes through women like a fast-food chain goes through paper napkins. So why were you the one who ended up engaged to him?"

Chelsea sighed. "Seth is so incredibly narcissistic that women tend to avoid him after a very brief exposure. One or two dates is usually enough, a few stalwarts make it to three. So much for his love 'em and leave 'em reputation. It's more the other way around. Seth is blissfully unaware of all that, though. He believes what he reads about himself, that he is an infinitely eligible, sought-after hunk."

"Which is why that column with its negative insinuations had such a powerful effect upon him," concluded Cole. "Okay, I can believe that women find his self-absorption intolerable. So why did *you* last longer than three dates with him? Why did he assume that *you* would marry him?"

How could she explain that the reason she'd been able to continue seeing Seth was because she didn't care that his primary relationship was with himself? She wasn't looking for love or affection or even companionship. She had been too busy trying to cope with the notion of Cole Tremaine in love with Carling Templeton.

The pain that streaked through her was wholly unrelated to her migraine. But a tiny flame of hope flickered in spite of it. Cole had kissed her today. During those all-too-brief moments in his arms, real passion had flared between them, as if it had lain dormant yet alive during their four-year separation. Cole wanted her; she'd felt the undeniable masculine evidence of his need. Did she still have a chance with him, despite the pernicious threat of Carling Templeton?

Her heart racing, she eyed him thoughtfully. "Cole, are you going to stay with me at your family's place in the mountains?" she asked with what she hoped was credible innocence.

He smiled. The trapdoor had just slammed shut. She was caught and she didn't even realize it. But he did. He savored his victory. "Yes, I am. I could use a vacation and the Catoctins have always been one of my favorite places."

She tried to look gratefully demure instead of triumphantly exultant. She would be alone with Cole while Senator Templeton's daughter was hundreds of miles away!

And as she'd already arranged a whole month away from work, her timetable was her own, to go and to be wherever she wanted.

In the mountains, she and Cole would have time to get to know each other all over again without outside interference or distractions. They could renew the bonds that had once bound them together, and rekindle the passion still smoldering between them.

Was a reconciliation possible? Her heart burgeoned with hope. She was four years older—and four years wiser—since her last go-round with Cole. She'd achieved her educational goals and had far more confidence in herself and her own strength and ability. She wasn't as threatened by Cole's dominance; she felt certain she could hold her own with him if necessary and compromise without feeling overpowered.

And she was still in love with him, she admitted to herself. A ribbon of heat twisted through her, making her feel warm and moist and sensuous.

"Cole, thank you for helping me," she said huskily, her eyes lambent, her smile sweetly alluring.

His smile was positively wicked. "Darling, the pleasure is all mine. Now lie down and get some rest."

Five

Chelsea, we're here."

The deep, masculine voice penetrated the thick fog enveloping her, and Chelsea tried to ignore it, preferring to drift languorously back to sleep. For a second or two, she wasn't sure where she was; she just knew that she was too comfortable to move or speak or even open her eyes.

"How's your headache?" the voice persisted.

She blinked. Her last memory was of a grinding pain in her skull before falling into a deep, drugged sleep. When she felt a big hand begin to stroke her hair, her eyes flew open. She was lying across the backseat of the limousine, Cole's suit coat tucked around her. He was next to her now, gently massaging her scalp with skilled fingers.

She stared at the dark material of Cole's trousers stretched taut across his muscular thighs. She was lying on her side facing him.

"Those pills really knocked you out." Cole's voice sounded above her. "You haven't moved for the past three and a half hours."

"I took four pills," she confessed in a sleepy, slurred voice. "I wanted them to work faster."

He frowned his disapproval. "You shouldn't screw around with medication dosages, Chelsea. Follow the directions printed on the prescription label, that's why they're there."

"You sound like one of the pharmacists employed by the Tremaine Drugstore Chain," Chelsea murmured, then closed her eyes again. She couldn't keep them open, she didn't want to.

"Our qualified pharmacists are the backbone of Tremaine Drugstores' phenomenal success..." He launched into the familiar company spiel, only to have her interrupt.

"No, the Tremaine business sense and marketing savvy—your father's and yours—are the backbone of Tremaine Incorporated's success," she mumbled with sleepy admiration, her eyes still tightly shut.

Cole stared down at her. What she said was true and he felt a certain pride that she recognized it. In the condition she was in, lecturing her about the pharmacological effects of incorrect medication dosages was clearly a lost cause, though he would've liked to continue—or better yet to have her argue with him. He needed some distancing diversion to put the brakes on this odd rush of tenderness surging through him as he gazed at Chelsea, flushed and drowsy, and now cuddling against him.

Her face was dangerously near his masculinity, which was burgeoning from the sweet proximity of her lips. His arousal had kept him in a state of restless discomfort during the entire drive through the mountains.

Reluctantly, he opened the car door and slipped outside. Chelsea murmured a sleepy protest; she wanted him to stay with her. Muttering an expletive, Cole tried to will away the lust pulsing through his body. She was drugged, out of it; she didn't know what she was doing. And they couldn't stay in the limousine for the rest of the day. Well, maybe *she* could, he conceded grimly, but not him! He needed a shower—a cold one—and a ferocious bout of exercise if he was ever to get any sleep tonight.

As organized as always, he unlocked the door of the house and carried Chelsea's luggage inside before returning to the car to scoop her up in his arms.

Barely awake, Chelsea turned her face into the curve of his shoulder and snuggled closer. The enticing male scent of him filled her nostrils and she sighed contentedly. She could feel the rippling strength of his shoulder muscles and the warmth of his big hands on her bare thighs.

He carried her inside, through the artfully appointed rustic interior of the main room to a small bedroom, decorated in pastel shades of pink.

When he laid her down on the bed, Chelsea opened her eyes and gazed drowsily at her surroundings. There was pink, pink, and more pink, all lace and ruffles. This was obviously someone's idea of the ultimate feminine room. As clouded as her mind was, Chelsea knew decorating overkill when she saw it.

"I feel like I'm in a Barbie doll's room," she murmured. "I've never seen so much frilly pink in my entire life."

Cole's lips twitched in amusement. "Dad had it decorated years ago for my cousin Karen's visits. She's his only niece and he adores her. Never having had any daughters, he had no idea what a young girl's room looked like, so he ordered the feminine works."

"I remember your cousin Karen," Chelsea replied, smiling up at him, her big brown eyes soft and languid. "I liked her very much." She almost added that she'd planned to ask Karen to be one of her bridesmaids when she and Cole married. Except that the wedding had never taken place and the invitation had gone unextended.

"Karen's married now," Cole remarked. "She's the same age as you are and she already has two cute little kids, a boy and a girl."

She would have had to have been totally comatose not to have felt the sudden tension emanating from him. But although Chelsea noticed that tension she was too relaxed from the powerful effects of the medicine to worry. "Does Karen still come here for visits?" she asked drowsily.

"Not anymore. She lives in California now and doesn't get back to D.C. very often. When she does, there is never enough time to come the whole way up here. This room hasn't been used for quite a long time. When my brothers or I bring a woman here, she stays in the master bedroom," he added coolly.

"With one of the masterful Tremaines, of course," said Chelsea with a dizzy little giggle.

Some small sane corner of her mind recognized that the mention of Cole sharing the master bedroom with another woman should upset her. But the medication had freed her of all anxiety; she was too lethargic to work up even a smidgen of jealousy. She rolled languorously on her side and gazed up at him through her long, dark lashes. She felt marvelously sensual and free, completely unfettered by any inhibitions.

"Are *you* going to share the master bedroom with me, Cole?" she heard herself ask. She felt so strange, as if she were dissociated from what she was saying and doing. Her mind was floating in a pleasant haze.

"Certainly," Cole replied, flashing his wicked pirate's smile. "But not while you're in a drugged stupor. I want you fully conscious and totally aware of what you're doing when you surrender to me. And you will surrender, Chelsea. Completely. I intend to make you mine so absolutely and unquestionably that you will be willing to take me on any terms I choose to offer."

Confusion clouded her velvety dark eyes. It was difficult to concentrate with her brain feeling as if it were wrapped in soft gauzy cotton. "Is that a proposal or a threat?" she asked thickly.

For the first time since she'd awakened, she wished she had her wits about her, sharp and clear.

"It's definitely not a proposal, baby. I'll never propose to you again in any way, shape or form. Maybe it's a threat," he continued, as if savoring the words with pleasure.

The pieces fell into place with astonishing clarity and he marveled at the order of it all. Why, it was as if he'd carefully plotted each step! He decided that perhaps he had, subliminally. After all, he'd followed her, then brought her here to teach her a lesson she sorely needed. Chelsea Kincaid was about to learn how it felt to want to belong to someone completely—and be turned away. To plead to share that person's bed, home and life—and be rejected.

"When you beg me to let you live with me—knowing that you'll never have the security of a marriage proposal in the future—I'll take pleasure in reminding you that you turned down the opportunity to marry me four years ago. That you had your chance with me and blew it." He sounded positively elated by the prospect.

Chelsea frowned. Something was very wrong here. If only she could summon the energy to get angry, because what she'd managed to piece together in her muddled mind seemed infuriating in the extreme. Unfortunately, in her drug-induced torpor, fury eluded her. Still, her feminine pride—although anesthetized—urged her to retaliate.

"Who says I'm going to beg you to let me live with you?" Her voice sounded sleepy, slurred and thick, totally lacking the verve and power that the question demanded.

"You will," Cole assured her.

"Will not," she mumbled. She was less than satisfied with her response. However, the ability to indulge in rapier-sharp repartee was definitely impaired while under the chemical influence of sleep-inducing drugs. Cole remained standing beside the bed, his restless energy penetrating her torpid state. He wanted to fight with her and she wasn't proving herself a very worthwhile opponent.

She summoned every ounce of her willpower to try again. "What about Carling?" Her sarcasm lost its intended effect when offered in a sleepy whisper. "What's she going to think about all this?"

"Let's just say that Carling and I have an understanding," Cole replied smugly.

"And understanding about what? Punishing your former fiancée? What sane woman would stand for that?" This was too bizarre and too exhausting to comprehend. And Chelsea closed her eyes, unable to keep them open for one more moment.

She stirred slightly when Cole sat down on the bed to remove her shoes. When he'd taken them off, she sighed softly and rolled onto her stomach, burying her face in the baby-pink bedspread-covered pillow. Soon she was sound asleep again.

"Chelsea," he called her name but she didn't move. Her breathing was deep and even.

Frustration coursed through him. He finally had her all to himself—and in a bedroom!—but she was completely inaccessible. If there were some invisible scoreboard keeping tally of the points scored in the battle between the sexes, Chelsea would have to be awarded this particular round, he conceded irritably. She'd won it hands down. For having been informed of his appallingly insulting retribution, she had calmly rolled over and gone to sleep!

* * *

It was dark when Chelsea awakened, and for a few moments she lay quietly on the bed and watched the soft lacy curtains billow in the cool night breeze that rushed through the open window. The full moon illuminated the room as effectively as a streetlight, casting shadows on delicate flowered wallpaper.

Her stomach rumbled a loud, protesting growl. She lazily cast an eye toward the electronic clock on the dainty bedside table. It read ten, reminding her that she hadn't eaten a thing since dinner the night before, over twenty-four hours ago. No wonder her hunger pangs were so insistent!

The veils of sleep fully lifted. Her momentary peace dissipated, along with her hunger, as awareness descended upon her with sledgehammer force. She was on the run from the Stricklands and their hired bounty hunters and from the *Globe Star Probe* along with every other newsperson in the entire world.

But that wasn't the worst of it. Chelsea covered her face with her hands and stifled a moan. She had turned to Cole Tremaine to help her, and oh, what a mistake that had turned out to be!

Now she was trapped on some godforsaken mountain; she didn't even have a clue as to where because she'd been asleep during the journey here. She'd willingly allowed Cole to spirit her away. Her whole body flushed with mortification as she remembered her dreamy delusions of rekindling a romance between them, while *his* sole purpose for bringing her here was to punish her, to humiliate her in retaliation for their broken engagement.

I intend to make you surrender so completely that you will be willing to take me on any terms I choose to offer. I'll never propose to you again. You had your chance with me and you blew it. His words rang in her ears. She might've been heavily drugged when he'd said them but they had made an indelible impression on her brain anyway.

Chelsea sat up abruptly, the rage she'd been unable to express earlier surfacing in a rush that was literally dizzying. She had to put her head between her knees and close her eyes to combat a wave of vertigo which suddenly overcame her.

A few minutes later Cole found her sitting up in bed, clasping her legs with her arms, tucking her head between her knees.

"Are you all right, Chelsea?"

He had the nerve to sound concerned. Chelsea grimaced. "Do I look all right? And what do you care anyway? After all, you're the creep who's been plotting and relishing my abject humiliation!" She slowly lifted her head to glare at him.

He had changed out of his executive power suit into a pair of faded, well-worn jeans and he'd rolled the sleeves of his white shirt to his elbow, leaving the first few buttons undone. Chelsea's eyes flicked over him, unwilling but unable to keep from noticing his broad shoulders, trim waist and flat belly. Involuntarily her gaze dropped to his powerful, muscular thighs and the way the soft denim conformed to the sizable bulge of his masculinity.

She caught her breath and swiftly looked away. "Just get out of my room, Cole Garrett Tremaine!"

Cole laughed. "Well, your color is still ghastly but you seem back to normal. Normal for you being feisty, outspoken and rebellious, of course."

"And it's a good thing that I am. It's a necessity when it comes to dealing with the likes of you!"

"No, Chelsea," he replied silkily. "I prefer my women docile, submissive and compliant. And you'll be all of those things after our little sojourn here in the mountains."

"I'll never be any of those things, not even if I were imprisoned in one of those indoctrination camps that specialize in brainwashing. So if you're expecting a—a passionate idyll here with an adoring sex slave, you'll have to look elsewhere, I'm afraid."

The memory of herself scheming to win him back by setting the scene she'd just reviled flashed through her unguarded mind. She blushed fiercely. It was too mortifying to contemplate!

"If you insist on holding me captive, you'll find yourself stuck with a bad-tempered, critical, sharp-tongued witch," she continued fiercely.

She cringed every time she thought of herself dreaming about him like a lovesick fool, actually looking forward to spending time here with him when all he wanted was to use her to avenge his oversized ego.

Are you going to share the master bedroom with me, Cole? The words echoed in her head. She'd actually said that to him! Chelsea fought the urge to scream. It wouldn't do to get all emotional and unhinged; that could only work to Cole's advantage.

"I'm curious about one thing, though, Cole." It took considerable willpower to play it cool, but she succeeded. "Why did you tell me the truth about why you brought me here? Wouldn't it have been easier—and more effective—to pretend that you wanted me back? To lead me on and trick me into falling in love with you again... and *then* laugh in my face and remind me that I'd thrown away the opportunity to marry you and could never have another chance?"

Yes, why hadn't he done that? Cole puzzled. That had been his original plan, but instead he'd warned her honestly about his insulting, offensive intentions. The honor of an Eagle Scout died hard within a man. But, of course, he wasn't about to tell her so.

"Tricking you would be too easy," he said with an arrogance that set her teeth on edge. "Since I've given you fair warning, your unconditional surrender will be far more satisfying."

"And that much more humiliating for me." She shuddered. She already knew the risks of falling in love with a man as demanding and possessive as Cole Tremaine. But to allow it to happen, knowing in advance that his goal was to punish her, would be devastating, not to mention stupid.

A streak of white-hot anger rallied her from the pit of depression into which she'd descended. She had many faults—too many!—but stupidity wasn't one of them. "To be forewarned is to be forearmed, so the saying goes," she said coldly. "Now that I know what you have planned, I'll never *surrender* to you."

She emphasized the word surrender mockingly, just to let him know that she considered the concept ridiculous.

"You will," Cole assured her. "And I'll be sure to remind you of this conversation when you do."

Chelsea seethed. "I'm not going to get involved in one of those stupid I-will-not-you-will-too arguments." She abruptly slid off the bed and stood up, swaying as the room spun around her. She immediately sat back down on the edge of the bed.

"Chelsea—" he began, but she instantly cut him off.

"I'm all right, just feeling a little light-headed, that's all. So please spare me any display of false concern. What I could really use is something to eat. I haven't had any food since dinner yesterday."

"And after all those pills..." Cole frowned, his voice trailing off. "Can you walk to the kitchen or do you want me to bring a tray to your room?"

Chelsea looked at him. He was serious. Was the same man who'd just gleefully revealed his plan to emotionally annihilate her now offering her room service?

"I'll go to the kitchen." Rising slowly this time, she walked unsteadily to the door.

"You still haven't gotten your sea legs," Cole observed. "I'll carry you."

"No thank you. I'd rather crawl on my hands and knees than accept any assistance from you." She stared out the door.

"On your hands and knees, hmm?" Cole chuckled rakishly. "I like that imagery. Maybe we could—"

"Maybe you could shut up!" she snapped. "I don't appreciate your adolescent, prurient humor. Oh!" She gasped as she was swept off her feet and into Cole's arms. "Put me down!" she demanded crossly. "I said I didn't want—"

"It doesn't matter what you do or don't want. I'm making the decisions here."

She wasn't feeling well enough for an all-out physical struggle. He was walking very fast and the sensations of speed and height unsettled her. Pure reflex caused her to clasp her arms around his neck and cling to him.

Their faces close, their expressions grim, both were silent as he carried her into the wood-paneled kitchen and set her down on one of the wooden benches lining a long, redwood picnic table.

Chelsea glanced around the kitchen. It was large and airy, done in shades of butterscotch and cream, and contained every appliance one could name. "At least its not pink," she muttered. Her eyes happened to meet his. She and Cole almost smiled at each other. Almost. Both quickly got hold of themselves and fixed their scowls firmly into place.

"We have our own generator, which supplies all our electricity since there are no power lines up here." Cole spoke first. The prospect of enduring a long, stony silence was not at all appealing to him. He'd been alone for hours. Now that Chelsea was awake and alert, he intended to interact with her.

Interact. He smiled inwardly. Now there was a pallid and inane euphemism for what he intended to do!

"Do you have one of those satellite dishes you mentioned earlier?" Chelsea replied politely, equally determined to keep a neutral conversation flowing. Hostile silences were not her forte either. "To get television stations from around the world?"

"We've had one for years. You'll have the pleasure of seeing the Jilted First Bridegroom on stations from New Zealand to Newfoundland."

Chelsea winced. "It won't bring me pleasure, Cole. You're the one who gets a kick out of premeditated humiliation, not me."

Cole felt heat rise from his neck to his face. No, he vowed silently, he would not let her make him feel guilty. "What would you like to eat?" he demanded gruffly. "We keep a fully stocked freezer, refrigerator and pantry. We've got anything you want."

"Good. I'll have braised eels, pheasant under glass and glazed kumquats with heavy cream."

"Hmm. It seems we have everything but that." Cole knew he shouldn't laugh but he couldn't help himself. She could be such a defiant brat. And while her outspokenness sometimes angered him, it just as often struck him as funny. "We happen to be out of that tonight. How about steak and eggs or ham and eggs or bacon and eggs?"

"If I were to make a wild guess that you have a surplus of eggs, would I be way off the mark?" Her brown eyes gleamed.

"There are four dozen in the fridge," Cole confessed. "Joe Mason—he lives in Babcock and comes up to check on the place every week or so and keep the supplies stocked and fresh—is always looking to save us money so he stocks up on store specials. There must have been a good one on eggs this week."

"Too bad Easter is so far away. We could dye them."

"As it is, we'll have to eat them—at least some of them. Joe takes home what we don't use. He has seven or eight kids so nothing goes to waste. Joe's a very industrious guy.

Keeping an eye on this place for us is just one of his many jobs."

"With such a big family, he needs a lot of jobs," remarked Chelsea. "Where's Babcock?"

"It's the nearest town, down in the valley about fifteen miles from here."

Chelsea's eyes widened in dismay. "The nearest town is fifteen miles away? Am I right in assuming there isn't any public transportation between here and there?"

"You're a hundred percent right, darling. There isn't a bus line deep in the mountains. You're here until I decide to let you go, Chelsea."

She sighed. "Can we take a break from the threats? I've starving. My blood sugar is so low I can hardly think. So let's raise it along with my cholesterol level. I'll have steak and two eggs, over easy. And two pieces of whole wheat toast with butter and strawberry preserves and tea with milk and sugar. Oh, and if you have any fresh peaches, I'll have a couple sliced in a dish with brown sugar sprinkled over them."

He stared at her. "Anything else?" he asked impassively.

A smile played around the edges of her mouth. "That'll be all, thanks. I'm sorry I can't help you prepare any of it. I'm afraid I'll get dizzy if I try to stand. After all, I could barely walk, remember? You had to carry me in here."

"I remember." He opened the refrigerator and various cabinets and began to set the items out on the long, wide counter. "You're lucky I can cook. Otherwise, it would be cold cereal for poor dizzy little Chelsea."

"You're quite a capable cook. I always admired the fact that your father didn't raise you and your brothers to be useless princes, unable to function without a staff of servants. You and Tyler and Nathaniel can do anything from sewing a button on a shirt to rebuilding an engine."

"The Tremaine men are self-sufficient. That's one of Dad's favorite sayings. He didn't want us to be a trio of pampered little rich boys."

"You're certainly not that." Chelsea propped her elbow on the table and rested her chin in her palm. She regarded Cole thoughtfully. "You dad is a very wise man. Unfortunately, without your mother around to moderate, he carried his child-raising theory to extremes. You and your brothers turned out to be *too* self-sufficient."

"There is no such thing as being too self-sufficient," Cole refuted, slapping the bread into the toaster.

"Well, maybe the word I'm looking for isn't self-sufficient. I think it might be *rigid*. Yes, that's it," she continued lightly. "You and your brothers have your own set ways of thinking and doing and seeing things and you can't accept or accommodate any conflicting views. What's odd is that's only in your personal lives. In the business world, you're incredibly flexible and pragmatic."

"I appreciate your compliment about our business style," Cole said dryly. He cracked the eggs into the frying pan with restrained violence. "But the rest of your analysis is absurd. You clearly don't know what you're talking about."

She grinned. "See what I mean?"

He threw the small strip steak into the pan. "No, I don't. Here." He thrust a glass of orange juice and a plate of toast in front of her. "You said yourself that your blood sugar was so low that you couldn't think and I agree. You're babbling on and on without making any sense at all. The sooner you get something into your system, the sooner you'll be capable of thinking clearly."

"And thinking clearly, of course, means agreeing completely with you."

"That's right," snapped Cole, expertly flipping the eggs.

Chelsea giggled. "I'd forgotten how much fun it is to tease you. You're hilariously dogmatic."

"That's an oxymoron," Cole said stiffly. "Aren't good writers supposed to avoid them?"

"Ah, here it comes. The attack on my career." Chelsea heaved a resigned sigh. "I'll save you the energy and do it myself. I know all your lines. Not only am I a poorly paid staff writer for a useless magazine with a too-small circulation, I also write badly. But let's not stop with my career. I know you must have some other observations to share about everything that's wrong with my life."

He placed the plate of steak and eggs in front of her. "I suppose I could mention that your unimpressive salary forces you to live in a two-room efficiency in an aging and dreary apartment complex. And because of Washington's surplus of single women and shortage of eligible men your dates were few and far between until you managed the stunning feat of getting yourself engaged to Seth Strickland."

"Whereas if I'd married you when you ordered me to, we would now be divorced and I'd be an unskilled woman working at an even lower paying job—one I'd have had to take regardless of its lack of interest and satisfaction for me because I desperately needed it." She paused to take a bite of the food.

"This is delicious," she remarked before continuing calmly, "I'd be living in an even worse apartment complex, a dangerous one with cheap rents and big roaches and a high crime rate, while I struggled to support myself and our emotionally traumatized children who would spend their days dumped in cheap day care or, when they got older, entirely on their own because I'd be working. Naturally, I couldn't stay at home with them when they were sick, because I couldn't afford to miss a day's pay."

Startled, Cole looked up from the peaches he was slicing. "I'd never permit my children to live in some rat trap and be dumped in cheap day care all day—or to be left unsupervised!"

"Then not only would I have a pitifully low income, substandard housing and unhappy children, I'd also be involved in a custody fight with you." She shivered. "That was my mother's life and the one I lived as a young kid. From the time I was old enough to think, I promised myself I wouldn't repeat the experience."

Cole placed a teapot, sugar bowl and small milk pitcher on the table, along with two cups. He sat down on the bench opposite her while Chelsea poured them some tea.

"When I met you, you were living in the suburbs with your mother and stepfather and Stefanie and your two half-brothers. Your home was a decent-sized tract house in a pleasant enough neighborhood," he said quietly.

"Oh, our living conditions improved greatly when I was sixteen and Mom married Jack Emerson." Chelsea heaped sugar, then splashed milk into her tea. "But after my parents' divorce when I was five, and Stefanie was two, Mom, Steffie and I ended up in the kind of crummy apartment complex I just described to you. My mother had me when she was only nineteen and was a full-time housewife until the divorce. She didn't have any job skills—she couldn't even type—so she was glad to land a job in the kitchen of a hospital as a dietary aide. Unfortunately, it was shift work and it didn't pay much. We were always broke. Stefanie and I used to dread the end of the month when the bills started arriving."

"What about your father?" demanded Cole. "He's a chemical engineer, he earns a good salary. Why didn't he pay child support?"

"Oh, he paid the court-ordered amount, which wasn't all that much. It certainly was not enough to fully support us. He lived a very different life-style. He bought a house and always had a new car and money for all the extras. Visiting him was like stepping into another world for Stefanie and me. He bought us nice clothes and toys but he insisted they be kept at his place. We weren't allowed to ever bring anything home. And he was always reminding us that we could leave that dump and our mother and come live with him."

"That wasn't fair!" Cole protested indignantly. "Trying to bribe kids into living with the parent with the most money is reprehensible."

"I always thought so," Chelsea agreed. "And Stefanie and I refused to be bought. But my dad isn't the total villain, either. Mom could be incredibly vicious and vindictive. She was very clever at sabotaging Dad's scheduled visits and blaming him for all our problems. They both went to any lengths to retaliate against the other, so we had the court fights and the kidnappings..." She shrugged. "It was imperative for me to get an education and be able to support myself and any children I might have without having to depend on some man who might use money as a weapon against us."

"Some man." Cole took a long swallow of his plain, dark tea. "But that was me at one point, wasn't it? And you saw me with all the money and power and you with none."

"I guess it was something like that. I didn't have much confidence in myself back then. I needed those degrees like some kind of magic talisman. I had to know I could get a decent job." She tilted her head and a proud smile briefly crossed her face. "I know you don't think much of the magazine or my position on it, but I've made some valuable contacts through it. If I were to desperately need more money, I could find another job that paid more without any trouble. But right now, I'm satisfied where I am."

For the next few minutes, they sat in silence, Chelsea eating the meal with real relish, Cole watching her with narrowed, intent eyes. "You're not a bad writer," he said at last, his voice so low she almost didn't hear him.

Six

Chelsea laid down her fork and stared at Cole, bracing herself for the sarcasm she was certain would follow.

But no scathing barbs were forthcoming. He just stared moodily into his teacup. "And the magazine's not so bad, either," he said at last. "The circulation would improve if it had better distribution."

Chelsea's astonishment grew. "That's true. But the Tremaine Drugstore Chain, the largest in the D.C. area, doesn't carry *Capitol Scene*, and neither does Tremaine Books," she reminded him.

"That was my decision." Cole met and held her gaze. "The day you were hired by *Capitol Scene*, I issued an order that the drugstores and the bookstores were no longer to distribute the magazine."

He waited for her to explode. True she'd finished the food, but she could hurl the china at him or scald him with the tea still left in the pot. Part of him admitted that he'd have it coming. He'd just confessed to sabotaging her beloved magazine as a personal vendetta against her. She had a right to be furious and retaliate.

Naturally, he would fight back.

Chelsea sat unmoving, staring down at her plate. When she lifted her head, he was shocked to see her eyes filled with tears.

"You must really hate me," she said softly. She swallowed hard. "But I can't blame you. After what I did to you four years ago and to Seth today. . ." Her voice broke on a small sob. "I say that I don't want to hurt and humiliate others, but I seem to do it anyway. So what kind of a person does that make me? A cruel one, a deceitful and self-deluded one. A user, a hateful one."

She stood up, nervously running her fingers through her thick auburn hair. Her hands was visibly shaking. "If—if you'll excuse me. I—I'd like to go back to my room now."

Cole stood up, too. "You're not excused."

"I have to be alone!" She turned and hurried from the kitchen.

He was right behind her and caught her easily. "What the hell's going on?" he exclaimed roughly, gripping her by her upper arms and forcing her to face him. "I thought you'd be infuriated and instead you burst into tears!"

"Cole, please let me go." Her voice shook. Her lips quivered. She was fighting a desperate battle not to sob and clearly on the verge of losing it.

"And you're not upset because of Tremaine Incorporated's failure to carry *Capitol Scene*. That might be worth shedding a few tears over since it does cost the magazine revenue." Cole was incensed. "Instead, you're crying because you think it's all your fault, that you *made* me instigate the boycott. You're crying because you just assassinated your own character and you actually believe that your stupid armchair analysis, which I've always tried to warn you against, is true!"

"You don't understand!" Distraught, she tried to pull away from him.

He only tightened his grip. "No, you're the one who doesn't understand. It took courage not to let yourself be pushed into that wedding today, you little idiot." He gave her a small shake. "It would've been cruel and deceitful to have gone into it knowing how wrong it was for you both. The same applies for our engagement. I'm not an easy man to say no to, Chelsea, but you did it because you felt it was right. That doesn't make you a hateful user."

Chelsea's mouth dropped open. Her tears abruptly dried up; she was too astounded to cry or to utter a single word.

Cole released her and stepped away, rubbing the back of his neck in a gesture of frustration and irritation. "In light of your personal history, you did the only thing you could do. And you were right in thinking I'd be the type who would wage a world war when it came to custody of my children in a bitter divorce."

He made an exclamation of disgust. "Yeah, I can see me running the entire gamut: bribery, withholding support money, kidnapping, court fights. I suppose I should thank you for sparing my kids all that."

Chelsea stared at him. She now knew exactly how Alice in Wonderland had felt at the Mad Hatter's tea party. Disoriented was too mild a word for her current state of mind. She felt obliged to say something, but what?

"This is the most bizarre conversation we've ever had," she managed at last. "You're defending me—to myself. But why?"

"Because I am, okay?" Cole replied testily. "And don't you dare get weepy and sniffle that I'm too kind and you don't deserve it. Even if it is true."

"I wouldn't dream of it." She grimaced wryly. Maybe she was already dreaming this entire surrealistic scene.

He felt as confused as she looked. "There's no need for a long, convoluted explanation," he added belligerently, "because there is none. When I told you why *Capitol Scene* isn't sold by the Tremaine stores, I thought I'd launched a helluva quarrel. I was fully prepared to catch every plate you threw at me but you—"

"Didn't give you the fight you expected," she finished, perception dawning. "Or was it the fight you *wanted*? My fighting spirit was broken and you couldn't stand it!"

Her big, dark eyes were shining. "So you restored it, you comforted me. You hated seeing me filled with self-doubt and recrimination. You want me to be strong and to stand up to you, especially when you know you're outrageously out of line." She could hardly comprehend that amazing flash of insight, but she knew she was right.

"Don't try to kid yourself into believing that I'm some kind of sappy, sensitive hero, Chelsea," Cole said coolly. "Remember why I brought you here? Well, all of that still stands. You can't beguile me into abandoning my plans."

"Can't I?" Chelsea arched her brows. "I wonder." Daringly, she moved closer, until she was standing directly in front of him. She laid her hands on his chest and lifted her head to gaze up at him.

They stared at each other for a long, charged moment. A dark blue flame burned in his eyes and she felt the effects of that heat streak through her. Her belly grew warm and that warmth spread upward to her breasts, making them swell. Without pausing to think, she slid her arms around his neck.

The action brought them close, so close that her breasts impacted against the muscular width of his chest. She felt the hard power of his tumescence against her. Her head began to spin but not from any painkilling drugs. The time her giddy whirl was purely sensual in origin.

"Are you sure you know what you're doing, little girl?" Cole rasped. "Because if you're not prepared to finish what you're starting, you'd better call it quits right now."

"What is it you think I'm starting?" Chelsea demanded with as much dignity as she could muster.

"This." Suddenly his mouth was hot and urgent against her neck. He tasted her with his tongue, then gently nipped the sensitive skin with his teeth. His lips kissed their way higher, finally reaching her mouth and claiming it in a long, deep, dominating kiss.

They were both breathless when he finally ended the kiss. But he didn't take his mouth from hers, choosing instead to nibble on her lips between short staccato kisses.

"You want me," he stated huskily, speaking against her lips. It was as if he couldn't bear not to have his mouth touching hers. "Badly."

"Yes," she admitted. A shiver tingled along her spine. He wouldn't let her mouth leave his, and it was incredibly sexy to talk while their lips were touching. "And you want me just as much."

She felt Cole's hands close around her bottom and settle her against his hard masculine contours. Chelsea moaned and arched closer. The throbbing heaviness, the urgency of his arousal pulsed intimately against her loins making her feel empty and restless and eager to be filled. It had been so long . . . too long.

"I'm going to have you." Cole's voice rang with triumph. He was the conquering male, relishing his victory.

And if there was a victory, it naturally followed there was a defeat followed by a surrender. Chelsea was not so far gone as to forget Cole's nefarious revenge.

"You won't if you're still playing your stupid games," she murmured breathlessly. Call it off, she silently pleaded. Tell me that what's past is past and tonight we're going to begin all over again. As lovers and friends and equal mature partners. "I'm not a bed-hopper and I'm not about to hop into yours for all the wrong reasons."

She felt him smile slightly against her lips. "That's my Chelsea. Feisty and outspoken right down to the wire."

Chelsea stroked his nape and teasingly touched the tip of her tongue to his. "You like me that way. You'd be alarmed if I were to become totally docile and submissive."

"You're so wrong, I'd love it," he insisted. "And it's going to happen, baby." He moved his hips, rocking intimately against her.

The heat between her legs built and spread through her whole body, until every inch of her was aching for his touch. It took great determination to pull herself out of his arms, but she did so. "No," she said softly. Her dark eyes were shadowed with pain. "And if that's what you think this is all about, then we'd better stop right now."

Frustration coursed through him. He couldn't let her go now. They were so close, he wanted her, *needed* her, desperately enough to come up with a compromise. "Tonight we'll call a truce," he said hoarsely. "No games, no revenge, no punishment. Tonight it's just you and me, wanting each other. Making love strictly for pleasure, with no ulterior motive except quenching our desire."

"No games, no revenge, no punishment and surrender," she repeated slowly. No love, either, she added silently, and her heart seemed to drop to her stomach. "You're proposing that we use each other for sex."

She was aghast. It sounded so cold-blooded and animalistic. The finer, higher human emotions of love and respect wouldn't enter into it.

"That's right, darling." Cole caught her to him again, fastening his hands around her hips, massaging the sleek hollows with deft fingers. "Tonight, it's strictly straightforward sex between two consenting adults who've shared a past and want to enjoy themselves now, in the present." His voice was as smooth as silk.

But its effect on her was the equivalent of pouring gasoline into a fire, and passion transformed into an equally hot anger. "Is that the kind of line you use now that you've evolved into a slick, fast-talking smooth operator?"

She closed her fingers around his wrists to remove his hands from her, then gave him a hearty shove to push him away. "Well, here's some friendly advice from someone who's shared a past with you but doesn't care to *enjoy* herself with you in the timeless present. Unless your partner is brain dead, don't tell her that you're using her strictly for temporary, selfish, meaningless sex. There is no bigger or faster turnoff."

For a moment, he was stunned speechless as he watched her stalk away. It had all happened so fast. One moment he'd been euphorically contemplating taking her to bed and the next....

By the time he recovered, she was halfway back to the pink bedroom. "Chelsea!" he roared and started after her.

She began to run. She made it into the room first, slamming and locking the door behind her.

"Chelsea, open this door!" Enraged, Cole began to pound on it. "I will not tolerate being locked out of a room in my own house. Let me in!"

"Your big-bad-wolf routine is getting old fast, Cole," she called, her voice cool and maddeningly condescending. "As long as I'm your *guest* here, this is my room and you have no particular rights to it. Now go away and leave me alone. I'm going to take a shower and then go back to bed and try to sleep. I suggest you do the same."

He stood on the other side of the door and listened to her open and close the inner door to the connecting pink bathroom—and lock it. The click seemed to reverberate in his skull. The sound of the shower being turned on, of the water beating down, further inflamed him. He was beyond mere anger; he'd ascended somewhere to the high planes of rage.

No one had ever been able to infuriate him the way Chelsea Kincaid could. No one had ever made him as happy or as crazy, had fascinated him, obsessed him the way she did. The irrefutable lock she had on his emotions was both irrational and unfair, he railed inwardly. Dammit, she knew how much he wanted her. And if she were aware of the power she held over him, she must be glorying in it.

The notion was intolerable. Cole stormed from her door into the enormous, wood-paneled room which served as the cottage's combined living room and family room. He strode straight to the mahogany sideboard where a lead crystal decanter filled with the finest single malt Scotch was placed. Snatching one of the tumblers beside it, he splashed the Scotch into the glass and gulped it down. The dark amber liquid burned a fiery trail all the way from his throat to his stomach.

The last time he'd been this angry with Chelsea was the day of their engagement party. No matter how he'd coaxed and cajoled, ranted, raved, bullied or threatened her, she hadn't caved in. He was grimly aware that if he were to try any or all of the above methods to get her into bed tonight, he'd also meet with failure.

The Scotch had a calming effect on his brain, enabling him to approach the problem with the Machiavellian style that served him so successfully in the business world.

Four years ago, he had walked away from Chelsea in defeat because she hadn't backed down from his demands that their wedding date be set six weeks from the day of their engagement party.

But tonight he was not going to lose. He'd once made a major tactical error that he was not going to make again. Tonight, he was going to tell her exactly what she wanted to hear. After all, according to Machiavelli's classic text of strategy, the end justified the means. And the means of getting her into bed was using words of love.

"I'm not a bed-hopper and I'm not about to hop into yours for all the wrong reasons." Chelsea's words echoed in his head. He'd known that all along; his big mistake had been being honest about his intentions. Well, his inner Eagle Scout could just stuff it, from now on he was playing to win. In this case the end *certainly* justified the means.

With a smile on his lips and an unholy gleam in his blue eyes, Cole went off to find a hammer and screwdriver. They were the ideal tools for removing a door from its hinges.

The bedroom was dark when Chelsea emerged from the pink tile and marble bathroom. She shivered a little as the cool night air drifted over her skin, which was flushed and rosy from her hot shower. She made a mental note to close the window before getting into bed and adjusted the big pink bath towel around her to ward off the chill.

Earlier, Cole had placed her suitcase on a small luggage rack near the wall. She snapped it open and fumbled for her nightgown.

The moonlight streaming through the fluffy pink curtains provided enough light to see, so she didn't bother to cross the room and switch on the bedside lamp. She took out her blue slip-style nightgown and dropped the towel before pulling the nightie over her head. The cool silk and lace felt sensuous and soft against her skin.

She closed the window and padded toward the bed with a resigned sigh. She wasn't tired at all; she felt wired and restless with energy—and with frustration, she conceded to herself. Her body was still humming with arousal, still yearning for the completion and satisfaction denied by the abrupt cessation of Cole's lovemaking. The shower had invigorated rather than relaxed her, and her long nap earlier

FREE! gold-plated chain

You'll love your elegant 20k gold electroplated chain! The necklace is finely crafted with 160 double-soldered links and is electroplate finished in genuine 20k gold. And it's yours FREE as added thanks for giving our Reader Service a try!

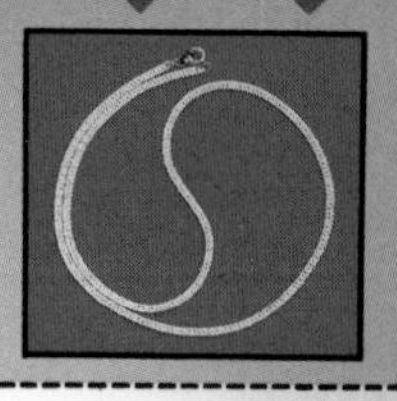

FREE-OFFER CARD

4 FREE BOOKS

FREE GOLD-PLATED CHAIN

FREE MYSTERY BONUS

PLACE HEART STICKER HERE

FREE-HOME DELIVERY

FREE FACT-FILLED NEWSLETTER

MORE SURPRISES THROUGHOUT THE YEAR—FREE

☑ **YES!** Please send me four Silhouette Desire® novels, free, along with my free gold-plated chain and my free mystery gift as explained on the opposite page.

225 CIS JAZH
(U-SIL-D-08/90)

NAME ______________________________

ADDRESS ______________________ APT. ________

CITY ______________________ STATE ________

ZIP CODE ______________________

Offer limited to one per household and not valid to current Silhouette Desire® subscribers. All orders subject to approval. Terms and prices subject to change without notice.

SILHOUETTE "NO RISK" GUARANTEE

There is no obligation to buy—the free books and gifts remain yours to keep. You receive books before they're available in stores. You may end your subscription anytime—just write "cancel" on your statement or return your shipment of books to us at our cost.

PRINTED IN U.S.A.

MAIL THE POSTPAID CARD TODAY!

eliminated any pressing necessity for sleep. Chelsea sighed again. It was going to be a long, long night.

The bedside lamp, shaped like a ceramic doll in an elaborate pink gown and topped with a ruffled shade, was suddenly snapped on. The pink light bulb bathed the room in an odd other-worldly glow.

Chelsea uttered a startled little shriek. Cole was stretched out on the bed, on top of the pink covers, watching her with hot blue eyes. "Cole!" she managed to squeak.

"Of course it's me." He smiled lazily. "You were expecting Seth Strickland? Or the *Globe Star Probe* team?"

"I wasn't expecting anybody! How did you get in here?" One glance at the open doorjamb gave her the answer to her question. He'd removed her door! She could see it propped against the wall in the hallway.

"Cole, you have to leave." Her voice sounded nervous and shaky. He'd completely unbuttoned his shirt and when he sat up in bed, the muscles in his chest, his arms and shoulders rippled and flexed. He looked big and powerful and strong. Chelsea gulped. She was painfully aware that if he didn't want to go, she had no way to make him leave.

"Chelsea." He reached out and grabbed her wrist, pulling her to him with unyielding force. "Don't send me away, darling."

He pulled her down onto his lap, his arms closing around her like steel bands. Instantly, reflexively, Chelsea tried to get up—and found that she couldn't move. "Cole, no!" she cried, her heart thundering wildly.

His lips brushed her cheek, her forehead, her hair. "Darling, yes." His hand slid possessively over the smooth curve of her stomach and the warmth of his palm kindled a fire in her belly that rapidly spread to the secret, innermost part of her.

"I couldn't stand to be away from you any longer, Chelsea. I decided to stop fighting myself and admit to you . . ."

He paused and drew a deep breath. "Admit to you that I never stopped caring about you. That I haven't stopped wanting you, and that letting you go four years ago was the worst mistake of my life."

"Cole!" Chelsea gasped, her dark eyes huge with astonishment. And blazing with hope. "Cole, do you mean it?" she heard herself say in a ragged, faraway voice. Automatically, her arms encircled his neck and she swayed into him.

"I couldn't carry on with my angry charade any longer." He blazed a trail of hungry little kisses along the sensitive curve of her throat. "It could never be strictly sex between us, Chelsea."

He cupped the swollen softness of her breasts, watching his hands mold the ice-blue silk over the shapely round globes. Her nipples were already pointed and hard and he placed his mouth over one, dampening the silk as he laved it with his tongue. He traced small circles around it, until it pulsated against the cloth, tight and distended. Then he treated the other nipple to the same massage.

Liquid fire burned through Chelsea's veins. She cried out as she squirmed on his lap, causing Cole to groan with urgency. She could feel the throbbing fullness of his masculinity hard against her and she quivered with arousal. There was something irresistible in the power of his need for her. Only with Cole had she ever felt the primal feminine need to give and give, until the giving became submission, surrendering herself to him and becoming part of him. Only with Cole had she wanted to yield her separateness and merge with another.

She felt that way now.

"I want to make love to you, Chelsea," he gasped. "In the full sense of the word."

His mouth opened hotly over hers and his tongue slipped inside, probing, rubbing, stroking in an excruciatingly sexual simulation. She responded with all the aching love, passion and tenderness she'd been saving for him, since that dark day four years ago, when they'd split up.

"I'm so glad you came back, Cole," she whispered, gently caressing the hard, tanned column of his neck with her lips. "You sounded so cold and callous before. As much as I wanted you, I couldn't go to bed with you, thinking that you'd just be using me."

"I know, baby." He nibbled the soft lobe of her ear, his breath warm against her. "I said all the wrong things out of spite. Now I'm saying all the right ones and we're going to be together tonight after all."

He stood up with her in his arms and headed out of the little pink bedroom. His body was pulsing with a need so powerful that it far surpassed simple desire. He wanted her with every fiber of his being.

"Are we going to the master bedroom?" Chelsea asked dreamily. She gazed up at him through her thick, long lashes, a delicious syrupy languor filling her, making her feel pliant and wonderfully weak.

"Most definitely." Cole smiled down at her. "That pink little girl's room is not conducive for sex, uh, loving." He cleared his throat and swallowed convulsively, appalled at his verbal blunder. If she picked up on it...

But Chelsea, grinning at the image of Cole in the small pink bed in the frilly pink room, had missed his telltale Freudian slip. She stroked the hard line of his jaw with her fingertips. "Oh, I don't know." Her eyes sparkled with teasing lights. "I thought you looked charming against the ruffled pink coverlet. I've never seen you in pink before and I think it looks very good on you. It might just be your color."

He uttered a pained and heartfelt protest, and they both laughed.

He carried her into a huge, masculine bedroom, all beige and chocolate brown and rich, dark wood, and laid her down on the king-sized bed. She smiled up at him. "You've been carrying me around all day. In and out of the car. Into the house, into the kitchen, into the bedroom."

He shrugged out of his shirt and began to unbutton the fly of his jeans, one thick metal button at a time. His gaze held hers. "I especially like where this last trip ended."

"I do, too, Cole," she said softly.

She watched him as a voluptuous rush of emotion surged through her. "Cole, this is like a dream coming true for me. Being here with you, knowing that you feel the way I do."

She was so in love with him; it was hard to remember a time when she hadn't loved him and wanted him. For four long, lonely years she had been by herself because no other man had captured her heart and ignited her passion. She would not settle for anything or anyone else. There was only Cole, just Cole.

His jeans, then his briefs, dropped to the floor. When he moved toward the bed, Chelsea welcomed him with open arms. Naked and virile, he came down on top of her and she sighed and wriggled under the full warm weight of his body. She couldn't hold back the words a moment longer. "I love you, Cole."

Her words echoed in his head, the aching feminine need in her voice intensifying his own urgency. His senses were filled with the scent of her, an enticing combination of soap and powder and woman. He felt the supple warmth of her skin. And he was hungering—starving—for the taste of her.

His mouth covered hers, and they kissed and kissed, deep, moist, ardent kisses that grew longer and hotter. More intimate. More intense. Cole ran his hands possessively over her, sensually relearning all her slender curves and womanly softness.

When he lifted her slightly to facilitate removing her nightgown, she cooperated with an eagerness that made him smile. "I remember the first time I undressed you," he murmured softly, his eyes sweeping over her nakedness with warm approval and appreciation of her body. "We were in the living room of my apartment—"

"On that enormous black-leather sofa," Chelsea cut in, her face aglow. Cole's rapt expression as he gazed at her, thrilled her.

She felt the warm strength of his hands cupping her breasts, his thumbs caressing her nipples. They were so sensitized that the tingling pleasure almost bordered on exquisite pain. She moaned deeply.

"You were so nervous," Cole reminisced, gliding his hands along the length of her rib cage to the indented hollow of her waist. "You told me it was the first time anyone had seen you naked since you were a little girl. You were modest and shy and inhibited." He circled her navel with his finger and she shivered with response. "And so very sexy and sweet."

"You told me I was beautiful," Chelsea whispered, remembering. "And the way you looked at me, the way you touched me made me feel beautiful." She ran her hands over the solid width of his shoulders, reveling in their muscular strength. "You were so loving and considerate and patient. There was no shame or pain or regrets for me, Cole. You made it beautiful for me. Always. Every time."

She kissed him lovingly, tenderly, giving herself up to the warmth of the memories and the heat of her passion.

A mixture of anticipation and desperation surged through him. She felt so soft and sleek, so very right in his arms. Everything was different with Chelsea, he admitted, his mind clouding in a sensual haze. He'd experienced and provided pleasure while in the arms of other women, but only with Chelsea was there this overwhelming feeling of rightness, of true and binding unity.

He lifted his mouth from hers and gazed down into the dark depths of her eyes. "I want you too much," he said hoarsely. "It's too intense, too—" he gasped for air, trying to regain control of himself and his runaway feelings. This was not going the way he'd planned. He wanted his lust unencumbered by heavy emotional significance and here he was, practically drowning in sentiment.

"I know, I know," Chelsea said soothingly, cuddling closer. "I'm a little scared, too, Cole. It's as if our past has merged with the present. It's almost overwhelming."

"Yeah. All these *feelings* cluttering up everything." He sounded so indignant and put-upon that Chelsea burst into laughter.

"Oh, Cole, I do love you." She hugged him tight, still chuckling. "I can always count on you to be honest with me. You're so action-oriented but all these *feelings* need to be talked out. And though talking about feelings isn't your strong suit, you're definitely making progress."

Her fingers intimately encircled him and she felt his pulsing virility. "But you're getting impatient, aren't you, love?" she teased. "And probably worried that I'm liable to launch into a nice, long armchair analysis of our relationship."

She caressed him, delighting in the smooth, throbbing heat of him. Cole made a sound that was a combination of a laugh and a groan, and swiftly flipped her onto her back on the mattress, pinning her there with the full strength of his body.

"No more talk," he growled.

"And a lot more action?" Chelsea asked playfully, arching into him, rubbing her bare breasts against the wiry mat of hair on his chest. It felt wonderful and she closed her eyes as tremors pulsed through her. His thigh was high and hard between hers, exerting a sublime pressure against the soft feminine warmth of her. When he slowly moved it back and forth, shock waves of pleasure crashed through her.

She moved against him, clutching his shoulders with her fingers and lightly scoring him with her deep-coral polished nails. A soft gasp of pleasure escaped from her throat and she cried his name in yearning.

Cole laughed softly, enjoying her unrestrained responses to him. "You're so sexy, baby," he said in the deep, rough tones of arousal. "So uninhibited and responsive and honest. There's no faking or game-playing with you."

He paused, tensing, his eyes widening as the full import of his words hit him. She wasn't aware that he was playing games with her, and it seemed so... unfair. A spasm of regret twisted through him. But then Chelsea's hands were on him, all over him, exploring the hard length of his back, and his taut male buttocks. His mind exploded with a heady combination of pleasure and need.

He slipped his hand between her legs and Chelsea groaned as he caressed the silky skin of her inner thighs. Simultaneously, his mouth closed over one aching nipple and he began to suck gently.

The wild hot feelings churning inside her were almost unbearably exciting. She couldn't hold back her cry of intense pleasure.

Cole smiled at her sinuous movements, at her soft, sexy noises. She made him feel so proud, so irresistible, the supreme male whose lover yearns for—and is wonderfully satisfied by—his lovemaking.

His fingers tangled in the downy auburn thatch between her legs, then deftly parted and probed the moist, satiny folds within. He eased his finger deep inside her while continued to arouse her with the rhythmic pressure of his hand. When he felt her soft flesh clench reflexively around his finger, when he felt her heat and her wetness, a wild, primitive urgency exploded within him.

"Chelsea, baby, I can't wait any longer." His voice was husky and thick. "You're ready for me, darling. So very ready."

"Yes, Cole. Yes!" Chelsea heard a faraway moan and was vaguely aware that it was hers. Cole knew exactly how to touch her, knew precisely what she wanted, and he drove her higher and higher until the wildly pleasurable spirals of heat had intensified to frenzied heights. "Love me now, Cole."

With a low, sexy growl, he made a place for himself in the dark warmth between her thighs and thrust slowly, inexorably into her. Chelsea squeezed her eyes shut as she felt him fill her. It had been a long time and it hurt a little but she took some deep breaths and didn't make a sound.

"Sweetheart, am I hurting you?" Cole asked quietly. Inside her, a part of her, he was exquisitely aware and attuned to her every nuance. He lay very still, giving her body time to adjust to him.

"It's just that four years is a long time," she whispered. "It's okay, Cole. I'll be fine."

He kissed her deeply, tenderly, his tongue filling her mouth as he filled her body. Her rigid muscles began to relax and her body flowed with a hot honeyed warmth that accommodated his hard virile strength.

They both sighed.

"Better, darling?" he asked softly, stroking her hair with his big hand.

"Oh, yes, Cole," she breathed. "It's good, so good." Hot little ripples of pleasure radiated through her. She arched her hips, moving in counterpoint to his slow and easy rhythm, which swiftly built and grew harder, deeper, faster.

Sheathed deeply inside her, Cole felt all reason and control spin away. "Chelsea, you're so beautiful. So soft and hot and tight. You fit me perfectly." He punctuated his words with kisses.

And then there were no more words, only the mingling of their sighs and moans. They moved together in a primal, rapturous rhythm, desire and need joining into a surging life-force, his passion inciting hers and hers spurring his in a timeless cycle of giving and taking.

"You're mine, Chelsea," Cole rasped, the ultimate pleasure sweeping through him. Chelsea called out his name at the same moment, as convulsions of ecstasy erupted deep within her. All sense of time and place were lost as the rapture claimed them, bonding them in a wondrous union of body and soul.

Seven

Warm and mellow in the languorous glow of fulfillment, Chelsea and Cole lay quietly together for a long time in the dark cool room, their bodies still joined in the sweet aftermath of spent passion.

"Oh, Cole, I can hardly believe this is happening." Chelsea sighed, stroking his cheek, his hair with loving hands. She felt so very close to him.

"Believe me, baby, it's already happened." Cole's voice was deep and dazed. He felt marvelously drained and utterly replete, unable to move or even think. Not that he wanted to.

"Don't go to sleep on me yet," she teased lightly, nipping at his shoulder with her teeth. "We have some talking to do."

Cole groaned. "Oh no, spare me from a talkative woman after sex!"

She gave him a playful spank. "Lucky for you I'm too happy to take offense at anything, even that chauvinistic remark. Just don't make any more like it," she added, grinning at him.

"You're happy, hmm?" He gazed down at her kiss-swollen mouth and dreamy, languid dark eyes. She looked well-loved and sated. And so appealing that he felt his pulses quicken.

"Oh, yes, Cole!" She wanted to laugh and cry and sing for joy. Waves of sheer happiness were surging through her. "This has been the most amazing day of my life. It started in the pits of depression and yet, here I am, floating on Cloud Nine. Metaphorically speaking, of course." She kissed his neck, tasting the salty sweat on his skin and sighed contentedly. "Writers have to be careful using metaphors, you know. There's nothing sillier than a mixed one."

"You are in a chatty mood tonight," Cole observed dryly. "How do I shut you up, I wonder?"

She pretended to take offense and they launched into a mock wrestling match, laughing and teasing each other, alternately tender and rough. Though he'd felt almost insensate with satisfaction a little earlier, Cole found the idea of making love to her again tonight increasingly appealing.

He took her mouth in a long, lazy kiss.

"I love you, Cole," Chelsea whispered against his lips. She was lying in his arms, her head resting in the curve of his shoulder, one of her legs tucked between his.

Cole knew she wanted him to return her declaration of love. She expected him to. When he opened his eyes, he found her watching him, her velvety brown eyes shining with love.

Oh well, why not? he reasoned foggily. What were words, after all? He could give her those. There was no reason to put an immediate end to their interlude, particularly now that he was intent on prolonging it.

"I love you," he told her, while telling himself something else entirely: that they were both mature adults who were great together in bed and it was nothing more than that. She was simply mistaking great sex for true love and he intended to ultimately inform her of her mistake and set the record straight.

But not now. If he did, that radiant expression on her face would instantly be gone. The light in her eyes would fade and be replaced by sorrow. And then she might cry.

Cole shuddered. He couldn't face it. Not tonight. He didn't have the energy or the stamina; it had been a long, arduous day and he wasn't up to a wildly emotional scene. It had nothing to do with not wanting to hurt her or make her cry, he assured himself. Nothing at all.

"Then... we're sort of picking up where we left off four years ago?" Chelsea asked hesitantly. Part of her was afraid to trust in the dizzying euphoria of the moment; she needed clarification of her hopes and validation of her dreams.

"You mean another whirlwind courtship?" Cole sounded as uncertain as she. *Another whirlwind courtship?* Followed by what—another engagement? Cole was aghast that the prospect was so appealing to him. It wasn't supposed to be!

Chelsea took his answer—or the lack of it—as an affirmation. "Cole, there's just one thing." Her expression was thoughtful. "Or maybe I shouldn't refer to a *her* as a *thing*. Carling Templeton. Where does she fit in? You said you two had an understanding."

"I did say that. And I do," he replied in a deliberately supercilious tone. He silently willed her to get mad and thus extricate him from this discussion.

Chelsea giggled instead. "Are you being deliberately obtuse?" She climbed on top of him, straddling him. Her long red hair tumbled around her shoulders, the thick curls falling over her breasts, her pink nipples teasingly visible through some of the silky strands.

Cole stared at her, his breathing growing labored and thick. She was a gloriously sexy vision and his whole body was responding to the sight and the feel of her. His hands stroked her thighs, which were parted and open to him. Her skin was so exquisitely soft, yet the muscles were firm and strong.

Chelsea caught his hands and interlaced her fingers with his. "Cole, I told you everything about Seth but one thing. That the only reason why I ever agreed to go out with him in the first place was because of the rumors about you and Carling Templeton."

She lifted his right hand to her mouth and pressed her lips, then her cheek against it. "You see, I've kept track of your social life for the past four years. I know you went out with lots of different women and that always bothered me. But hearing that you were serious about Carling just seemed to kill something inside of me. After that, I didn't care what was happening to me or around me, until last night when it finally sunk in that I was actually expected to marry Seth Strickland."

Cole reached up and cupped her breasts. "Chelsea," he began thickly.

"I have to know if I'm the other woman, Cole." She leaned forward voluptuously filling his hands. Her voice was soft and sultry. "Or your only woman."

Cole gave a short, husky laugh. "If you didn't already know the answer to that, you'd be out of this bedroom like a shot."

"Please tell me, Cole."

She asked him so sweetly. And her great dark eyes were gazing at him adoringly. Cole groaned. "I promised Carling that I wouldn't tell another soul but—oh hell—I never envisioned a situation like this!"

He pulled Chelsea down to him, then rolled her onto her back and settled her beneath him. "Carling and I aren't seriously involved, we never have been. Our understanding is to pretend that we are."

Chelsea was delighted. She smiled, her face alight with pure joy. "But why, Cole?" She wriggled luxuriously under him, relishing the feel of his weight upon her.

"Senator Templeton is a pretty overbearing guy, used to getting what he wants when he wants it. And he wants his only daughter married, he wants grandchildren. The senator accused Carling of letting a slew of eligible men slip right through her fingers, so he decided to find a husband for her." Cole grinned. "And from Carling's description, the candidate for her hand is some looney-toon recluse who owns and lives on a big ranch deep in the wilds of West Texas. He's rich, though, and one of Templeton's most loyal supporters. A match made in heaven as far as the senator is concerned."

"And so Carling asked you to pretend you and she were involved to trick her father? To make him think that *you* were a potential suitable candidate for her hand?" Chelsea frowned. "It sounds very fishy to me, Cole. I think she made up all that stuff about her dad and the recluse rancher to trick you into getting involved with her."

"Believe me, honey, Carling no more wants me than she does the guy from West Texas. We were both quite safe from a commitment in each other's company."

"Impossible. I don't believe it." Chelsea shook her head. "How could she not want you? You're brilliant and generous and thoughtful and handsome and dynamic and—"

"Domineering, aggressive, forceful, opinionated and rigid," Cole added dryly. "Not even my money compensates for those character traits in Carling's book. She's quite frank in admitting that she wants a husband who'll let her go her own way, preferably one she can lead around by the nose. No, Chelsea, Carling doesn't want me anymore than I want her. But since we were seen together so often, the town gossips spread the word about us as a couple."

"So Senator Templeton stopped pushing the recluse as husband material for her." Chelsea nodded in understanding. "But, Cole, how did this arrangement benefit you?"

He shrugged. "I was sick of *dating*. Do you realize that I've been dating for almost two decades of my life? I'd had it with the getting-to-know-you patter of first dates, and the etiquette and expectations if you go out with someone more than once. Carling is charming and sophisticated, but too headstrong and independent for me. She and I knew exactly where we stood with each other, so it was a very comfortable relationship. End of discussion. I've already told you way too much."

He gave her no time to reply. His mouth opened over hers and her lips parted instantly for the hot, possessive penetration of his tongue.

"I want you again, Chelsea," he said roughly. "Now."

"Oh yes, Cole." She stirred against him, achingly aware of his thick masculine strength pressing against her moist softness.

He eased himself into her, filling her, stretching her, making her moan with pleasure. Chelsea lifted her hips in response to his thrusts, clinging fiercely to him, urging him closer.

He surged into her more deeply. "You're a little witch," he breathed. "You make me lose my head. There's never been anyone in my life like you."

"You love me," she whispered, as the delicious tension intensified. She could feel him deep inside her and the intimacy thrilled her. "You need me. As much as I love and need you. We belong together, Cole."

She verified her words with actions, loving him fully, passionately, without reserve, giving and receiving a wondrous pleasure that knew no bounds.

For the second time that night, their passion crested and swirled, sweeping them both away into the shimmering heights of rapture....

"I must be crushing you, baby," Cole mumbled sleepily a long time later and made a move to roll off her.

"No!" Chelsea tightened her arms and legs around him and held fast. "Don't leave me, Cole. We've been apart for so long. You feel so good, I don't want to let you go."

When she flexed her inner muscles to hold him more tightly inside her, he groaned with pleasure. "And I don't want you to let me go, darling."

Again and again, all through the night, Chelsea and Cole flowed in a timeless cycle of sleep and loving, of rest and passion, awakening to satisfy their seemingly never-ending need of each other, then falling into a deep sleep, sated and replete in each other's arms.

"Breakfast!"

Chelsea's cheerful voice was the first sound Cole heard. He opened one eye grudgingly. "What time is it?" he asked, his voice husky with sleep.

The thick chocolate-brown curtains had been opened. Sunlight flooded the room through the floor-to-ceiling windows, which comprised one wall of the bedroom. The view of the forest was breathtaking. The clear, windowed wall provided the illusion that the whole outdoors—the huge leafy green trees, the colorful wildflowers and all the rest of the mountain flora—was an extension of the room.

But this morning Cole ignored the scenery. He struggled to a sitting position and stared at Chelsea, who was carrying a tray of dishes and smiling warmly at him.

"It's nearly eleven," she said, setting the tray in front of him on the bed. Its four small bamboo feet gave it a secure base. "I woke up a little over an hour ago, but you were sleeping so peacefully, I didn't want to wake you. I hope you still like pancakes," she added. "I remembered that you like all different syrups so I put maple, blueberry and strawberry on the tray."

"Nearly eleven!" He was stunned. "I've never slept so late in my life!" And then he glanced down at the stack of perfect, silver-dollar sized pancakes on the plate, the neatly arranged bottles of syrup, the cup of steaming black coffee. It smelled delicious and he suddenly felt ravenous. "Thanks. You didn't have to do this." He took a sip of the coffee and sighed appreciatively.

"I wanted to."

She couldn't seem to stop smiling. It was a beautiful day and she'd awakened in Cole's arms. That chronic sense of loneliness and loss that had haunted her since the devastating breakup with Cole, which she'd sadly come to accept as an integral part of her personality, was gone. For the first time in four years she'd awakened feeling young, happy and truly free. She'd felt like singing while she showered and dressed in a pair of bottle-green shorts, a matching camp shirt and sturdy walking sandals. She'd felt like dancing as she ate her breakfast and prepared Cole's.

"I used a few of the eggs in the pancake batter," she said chattily, sitting down on the wide bed. "But we still have dozens left."

She watched him eat, her eyes warm with desire and affection. He looked sexy and unshaven. The beige sheet covering him to his waist and his broad chest with its thick dark mat was exposed to her ardent gaze. His hair was tousled from sleep and he was savoring every bite of the food she had prepared for him. She felt as if her heart would burst with love and happiness.

Cole was enjoying the breakfast, but he kept stealing covert glances at Chelsea as he ate. She looked bright-eyed and fresh and that particular shade of green was beautiful with her coloring and auburn hair. She'd pulled the long, thick curls back into a ponytail again. It was a practical, easy style and looked cute, but he was remembering that dark-red mane last night, when it had cascaded long and silky and free over her naked breasts. He took another long swallow of coffee, feeling as if his skin were on fire.

He laid down his fork. His hunger for food had been satisfied, but he'd worked up another kind of appetite that demanded fulfillment. "Take your hair down, Chelsea," he commanded in a low growl.

Her eyes met his and she correctly read the intent in them. She slowly lifted her hand to remove the thick green elasticized band. Her hair tumbled over her shoulders.

"Now unbutton your blouse and take it off."

She arched her brows. "I'm supposed to strip for you while you just sit there watching, like a sultan being entertained by one of his harem girls?"

"That's right." He smiled wickedly. "You accused me of harboring a fantasy about a passionate idyll with an adoring sex slave, remember?"

"And do you remember I threatened to turn into a creature from a waking nightmare instead?" She removed the tray and set it on the floor, then jumped on the bed and attacked him with a pillow. "Well, I'm here. Your playmate from hell!"

"Hey, quit that!" Cole tried to ward off the down-feathered blows, then grabbed the other pillow and launched a counteroffensive.

The pillow fight went on until they were both laughing too hard to continue. Declaring a mutual truce, they tossed the pillows to the floor and sank down on the mattress, breathless with exertion and laughter.

"We're carrying on like a pair of escapees from a branch of Psychotics R Us," Cole said, shaking his head. "If Tremaine Incorporated's board of directors could've seen their future CEO pummeling with a pillow—"

"Pummeling with a pillow. Good alliteration. But let's never invite the board of directors into our bedroom." Chelsea reached up to stroke his cheek. "This part of our life is strictly private, just between the two of us, and we can be silly or sad or sexy. Anything we want."

"We've been silly, let's skip sad and move ahead to sexy." He pulled her into his arms. "You were about to pander to my sultan-and-harem-girl fantasy..."

She loved the idea of serious, conventional Cole indulging in bedroom games and told him so. "You're loosening up, Cole," she teased. "Four years ago, you would never have *spoken* the word fantasy, let alone suggest one." She knelt up in the bed and slowly began to unbutton her blouse.

Cole watched her, his blue eyes hungry and intent. "I'm a different man from the one you knew—and dumped—four years ago, Chelsea."

"It's highly debatable as to who dumped whom four years ago." She removed her blouse, then hooked her fingers in the wide, elastic waistband of her shorts and pulled them off. "And I don't feel like debating the issue right now." She was wearing jockey underpants and a matching tank top undershirt, both made of soft pink cotton.

Cole scrutinized her with an exaggerated expression of mock disapproval. "The first thing we're going to do when we're back in D.C. is to go shopping for some lingerie. What you have on looks as if it was filched from a guy's gym locker."

"It's very comfortable," Chelsea protested laughingly. "If somewhat un-harem-girl-like. Is the fantasy hopelessly shattered?"

"We'll just have to create a new one." Cole pulled her down to him and kissed her, his mouth moving sensuously over hers.

Their loving was long and slow, their almost leisurely pace belying their clamoring passion. Today, they savored every touch, talking and playing with the ease and affection of longtime lovers. Which they were in a sense, Chelsea thought dizzily as he moved to cover her body with his own hard, powerful one. Everything between them was new yet paradoxically retained a comfortable familiarity.

She sighed with pure pleasure as she wrapped her arms and her legs around him drawing him into her body, into her heart, into her life. Their earlier languor suddenly accelerated to fever pitch, turning deliciously, ardently rough and building to a heated, shattering intensity....

The late-morning lovemaking filled them with a charged energy, an I-can-do-anything kind of feeling that demands action. Cole opted for working it off in bed, but Chelsea had other ideas.

"Since we're here in the scenic mountains, I'd like to see them," she exclaimed enthusiastically, sitting up, her eyes bright with exhilaration.

"Take a good, long look, honey," Cole invited, pointing to the window wall and the scene beyond. "And then come here."

Chelsea chuckled good-naturedly. "I'd like to see it from the outside. To *experience* it. Come on, Cole," she wheedled, tugging at his hand. "It's a beautiful day. Let's go for a walk."

He allowed himself to be persuaded. After a quick shower, he dressed in jeans and a crimson polo shirt, then snatched Chelsea's hand in his and led her outside. Talking and laughing easily together, they walked along the trace of a trail which wound between tall evergreens and thick-trunked oaks, maples, elms and other leafy green trees, stopping to examine whatever caught their interest. They came to a small creek, flowing over rocks as it twisted a path down the hill.

"This leads into a small lake," Cole told her. "More like a pond, really. Would you like to see it?"

She nodded and they followed the course of the stream for almost half a mile until it ended in a waterfall, cascading over a five-foot cliff of rock into a small mountain pool.

"Is it deep?" she asked.

"The deepest part is in the middle, about seven feet. The water temperature is icy. My brothers and I used to swim here when we were kids," he paused and smiled. "Kids don't mind turning blue with cold. Adults seem to outgrow such dubious pleasures."

Chelsea stooped down and stuck her fingers in the water. "It's cold, all right," she agreed with a shiver.

He took her hand in his to warm it. Chelsea gazed at the clear placid water and the surrounding view of mountains, trees and flowers. It was peaceful and utterly silent except for the rustling of the leaves by the light breeze and the occasional bird or animal noises. So very different from the constant rush and sounds of the city.

"It's beautiful here." She sighed softly. "It's as if we're the only two people in the world."

"The forest primeval. And you're a sexy little wood nymph." Cole picked her up and swung her around, feeling uncharacteristically playful and lighthearted. He couldn't remember feeling so young or so happy in years.

When he set her on her feet, Chelsea reached for him, wrapping her arms around him and hugging him. "I love you, Cole. Please never, never let me go again."

It was a heartfelt, impassioned plea that penetrated his very soul. Cole held her tight, shaken with the force and intensity of his own emotions. It was terrifying to feel this much; no woman had ever possessed him so totally and part of him resented it. Chelsea reached him on every level and he couldn't control the wide range of emotions she evoked within him. Adjusting to the reality of her power over him was not easy for a man accustomed to dominating, to controlling.

Slowly, he eased out of her embrace, his face flushed, his breathing thick. He reached down to pick up a small, flat stone and sent it skimming across the water. They both stared at the rippling circles it made.

"That was neat!" Chelsea enthused. "I want to try." She picked up a rock, a big one, and threw it in the pond. It sunk straight to the bottom with a wide, resounding splash.

Cole gave a yelp and jumped back as the icy water splattered him. "That's not the way!" he exclaimed. "You don't just *drop* it into the water. And you don't use a rock the size of a boulder, either. You need a small, flat stone, like this one."

He proceeded to demonstrate. The stone-skimming lessons continued for a long time, until Chelsea met with moderate success in her efforts. By the time they hiked back up to the house, both were ready for a light lunch. Cole grilled hot dogs on the charcoal grill on the patio, while Chelsea investigated the hot tub nearby.

"Does this thing work?" she asked doubtfully, removing the cover and staring at the big, redwood tub filled with water.

"Of course. Joe Mason keeps it clean and filled. Turn it on. It'll heat up and we can use it after we eat."

He teased her because she insisted upon putting on a bathing suit before joining him in the warm swirling, bubbling waters. He was all for plunging in nude and did so, but she donned her peacock blue bikini before climbing into the tub.

Cole's eyes swept appreciatively over her shapely figure as she lowered herself into the water. "You remembered to pack a bathing suit for sitting around the motel pool while hiding out from the Stricklands, hmm?"

Chelsea blushed. "That sounds so calculating and premeditated. But it wasn't, Cole. I always take a bathing suit with me anywhere I go so I just automatically stuck it in my suitcase...." Her voice trailed off and she gazed moodily at the swirling water cresting around her. "I'm ashamed to admit it but since I've been here, I've put Seth and the wedding out of my mind. All I can think of is you—and us. Oh, Cole, I'm so glad we're back together, but I wish it hadn't happened this way. I really do have to go back and face my family and the Stricklands. I can't stay in hiding while—"

"Relax, baby, your family knows where you are. I called your parents and Stefanie yesterday while you were sleeping off your headache. I also called the Stricklands to tell them you were with me. I strongly advised Seth to refute the phony hospitalization story and come up with a statement such as 'the wedding was cancelled by mutual consent due to personal reasons, which will remain personal.' I told him if he didn't release it, I would, acting as your attorney."

"What did Seth say to that?" Chelsea asked, her dark eyes anxious.

"What he *said* is irrelevant." Cole shrugged. "He'll *do* what I told him to and that's all that matters. He has no choice, especially since I hired away the team of detectives—and I use the term loosely—that he sent after you."

"The creeps in the black Lincoln who tried to grab me on the road? You hired them away from Seth?"

Cole nodded. "I called my brother Tyler yesterday and asked him to track down the name of the sleazy agency Strickland used. After that, we simply hired the goon squad at triple what Strickland was paying them. Their first act was to apprehend the *Globe Star Probe* duo who were hot on your trail."

"You were very busy while I was sleeping," Chelsea said slowly. "I don't know how to thank you, Cole. You've taken care of everything."

"Of course. I always do." Cole's hand snaked out to seize her wrist. "As for thanking me..." He pulled her down onto his lap. "I think we can come up with a way for you to show your appreciation."

The waters bubbled around them as she slipped her arms around his neck. Their mouths met in a long, deep, sweetly satisfying kiss and Cole's hand moved to the clasp of the bright blue bikini bra.

And then a loud, shrill ring pierced the air.

Eight

Startled, Cole dropped his hand. Chelsea jumped to her feet with a gasp. "What's that?"

"The damn phone!" Cole muttered along with a few other choice expletives.

"The *car* phone? How can we hear it here?"

"It's not the car phone. I didn't make all those calls yesterday on the car phone, Chelsea. We have a telephone in the cottage."

"But how can there be phone service here, way up in the mountains? There aren't any wires."

"The so-called wonders of modern technology." He sounded less than delighted with the technology that made such intrusions possible. "We have a radio telephone linked into one of the communication satellites."

Cole got out of the tub and strode nude from the patio, into the house, down the hall and into a room that was clearly an office. The phone was ringing insistently. He answered it. "Yeah?" Clearly, he was in no mood to practice correct telephone etiquette.

Chelsea had followed him. Now she paused hesitantly on the threshold of the office and watched him sink, dripping wet, into the big leather chair behind the desk, the phone in his hand. She wasn't sure if she should go or stay.

"Tyler, what's up?" Cole barked into the phone. "Then why the hell are you calling me here?"

Why was his brother Tyler calling? Chelsea stepped into the office. It didn't actually sound like an urgent family emergency. Cole sounded more irritated than worried.

And then he sounded downright aggravated. "They did *what*? Yeah, no. No! *Uh-oh!* None of your damn business! Look if you don't stop laughing, I'm going to hang up." A split second later, he did just that.

"He—uh—didn't stop laughing?" Chelsea surmised dryly.

Cole didn't reply. He slumped forward, catching his head in his hands.

"Cole, what's wrong?" Chelsea rushed to his side. "Why did Tyler call? Was it important? What was he laughing about?"

"Is this an official interrogation or are you simply playing your own game of Twenty Questions?" Cole snapped.

Chelsea stepped back. "You don't have to bite my head off. You're obviously upset and I'm concerned about you."

"Well, get ready to be upset and concerned on your own behalf, Chelsea. First, the two *Globe Star Probe* reporters managed to escape from the intrepid detective trio. God only knows what they'll do now that they're on the loose. But that's a minor worry compared to what Tyler found so hilarious."

Chelsea thought of Kaufman and Rodgers and the story they were undoubtedly concocting for the infamous *Probe*.

And that was only a minor worry? She gulped. "What did Tyler find hilarious?"

"The thought of you and me holed up in the mountains together without a package of condoms," gritted Cole. "Ty reminded me that the drugstore in Babcock keeps them hidden behind the counter and to make a purchase, you have to shout your request to Mr. Gibbons, the octogenarian druggist who's hard of hearing." Having dropped that bombshell, Cole stood up and stalked from the office.

As an exit line, it was unparalleled. Chelsea stood, riveted to the spot, dripping water onto the braided rug, too shocked to even think of following him. By the time she'd gathered her scattered wits and run after him, he was locked in the master bathroom, the water from the shower splashing heavily against the tiles.

Her heart was pounding in her chest, her mouth was dry. Last night...and this morning, too. Graphic memories tumbled through her brain, and not one contained a single recollection of birth control. The truth was, she hadn't given prevention a thought.

And, obviously, neither had Cole. He emerged from the shower, a thick terry robe wrapped around him. He ignored her as he dressed, pulling on underwear, jeans and a gray, black and red striped rugby shirt. He shoved the sleeves of the shirt to his elbows, finally looked at Chelsea and saw her watching him and heaved a deep sigh.

"I didn't—it never crossed my mind—I've never—Damn! I can't talk, I can't even think straight! This has never happened to me before, Chelsea. All I could think of was making love to you again. The possibility of any little consequences never entered into it. Not last night, not this morning."

He cleared his throat and a dark red flush stained his neck and spread to his face. "Is there any chance that you—uh—were prepared?"

She shook her head. "I haven't needed to think about—using anything with anyone. There hasn't ever been anyone but you, Cole."

His big hands clasped her shoulders. "Chelsea, I'm sorry. I never meant to put you at any risk. I'd never deliberately try to hurt you that way."

"I know. It's not your fault, Cole. Neither of us was thinking very clearly last night."

"*Or* this morning," Cole interjected grimly, as if one night of precautionless passion might have been understandable, but to extend it to the morning was unconscionable.

She tried to move closer to him, but he kept her literally at arm's length. She stared at him anxiously. "How did Tyler know that we," her voice lowered, "that we made love?"

"He doesn't know that we did. In fact, he assumes that we haven't. But he does know what we *don't* keep in stock around here. Last year Tyler himself had to make that embarrassing trip to the Babcock drugstore and holler his request to old Mr. Gibbons. Nathaniel and I have been razzing him about it ever since. So Ty was howling at the thought of his upright, conservative big brother having to do the same—or else going crazy staying celibate with you right here as an irresistible temptation."

"Tyler thinks that you find me irresistibly tempting?" Chelsea murmured softly. Cole's unwitting revelation made her pulses jump for joy.

Cole chose not to comment on that. He was still reeling from the shock of his unsuspecting brother's teasing. Tyler thought his ever-perfect, mistakeproof older brother would never take a woman to bed without taking precautions, no matter how desperate he was for her body. And until last night and this morning, he never had. Cole Tremaine was too fastidious, too controlled, too responsible to ever take such a risk.

But he had last night and this morning! And if Tyler hadn't called, it would have happened again, right in the tub. Chelsea Kincaid, after a four-year absence in his life, had swept back into it and turned him into an impetuous, reckless hothead, as irresponsible and out-of-control as a hormone-crazed adolescent.

Cole was furious with himself. And he was confused. The time he'd spent with Chelsea in the mountains was the most exciting and satisfying of his whole regimented life. Deep down inside, he knew he would do it all over again if given the choice or the chance.

Once more he was obsessed by this woman—or maybe he always had been and always would be. It was a formidable acknowledgement for a man who insisted upon self-control. Around Chelsea, he had neither. Cole flinched.

Chelsea had picked up the terry robe he'd discarded and slipped it over her bikini. "Cole, I was wondering why and how Tyler happened to consider me an irresistible temptation for you." She smiled at him seductively, invitingly.

Cole's lips thinned into a taut, straight line. "I was wondering the same thing," he said stiffly. It was disconcerting to think that his brother had been clued in to his obsession with Chelsea. Cole Tremaine made it a policy to keep his feelings strictly to himself!

Chelsea watched him. She understood the force of his tension. The ruthlessly self-sufficient, unerring and infallible Cole Garrett Tremaine wasn't supposed to ever have slips or lapses. In his self-accusatory eyes, not even a wildly emotional and passionate reconciliation was reason enough for unprotected lovemaking.

She had a feeling that anything she might say at the moment would only make him feel worse. It was time to give him a little space before trying to convince him that he hadn't committed a capital crime.

"Cole, I'm going to get out of this damp suit and get dressed." She left the master bedroom suite and walked down the narrow hall to the small pink bedroom. The door was back on its hinges; Cole had attended to that before lunch.

He was right at her heels. "Chelsea, you don't seem to realize the gravity of this situation. For heaven's sake, you might be pregnant!"

"Or I might not be," she replied calmly. "Chances are, I'm not, Cole. It's the wrong time of the month."

"Famous last words," Cole ground out. "I wonder how many times those very words have been followed nine months later with a little bundle of joy?"

Chelsea glanced at him as she entered the doll-like pink room. "I seem to recall you claiming that you wanted a big family. Six children, I believe. So why is the prospect of just *one* tiny bundle making you come unglued?"

"Because I intended to be married before I became a father! And not only is it irresponsible and harebrained for a man who is nearly thirty-five years old to get a woman pregnant out of wedlock, it's downright tacky!"

She almost smiled. "Well, there's a way out of your dilemma, you know."

"I believe I already told you that I wouldn't propose to you again, Chelsea," he said between clenched teeth. He would *not* yield on that! "One near-engagement to you was more than enough."

"Then we'll skip all that." She was irrepressible. "I'll propose to you and we'll elope. I couldn't stand anymore pre-wedding hoopla myself."

"Chelsea, get a grip on reality! Look at what's happened since I brought you here. You should be furiously accusing me of not loving you, of using you sexually to satisfy my lust and my need for revenge. Don't you realize what I've done to you? And on top of all that, you could be pregnant! You should be flying into hysteria."

"You're supplying all the hysteria this little melodrama can handle at the moment," Chelsea said wryly. "As for making accusations..." She shrugged. "I—I probably would be hurling them if I felt there were any just ones."

"You don't think it's possible that I was lying when I said I loved you?" His voice was low, but violent in intensity. "That I only said the words because I wanted more sex with you and knew I couldn't get it without the obligatory catchphrase? You don't consider the possibility that I was serious about making you surrender everything to me? Which I did, and very successfully, I might add!"

His blue eyes glittered oddly. "You admitted that you loved me and always had, Chelsea. You confessed that no other man has ever meant anything to you, that you'd marry me today if I were to ask. You even took the risk of pregnancy for me. That makes me the winner."

"The winner of what? We aren't in competition with each other, Cole. We aren't at war with each other, either." She stared at him, a terrible unease beginning to creep through her. "You didn't *make* me surrender, Cole. I gave everything willingly, of my own conscious volition, the words, my body, all of me. And—and I want to have your baby. Doesn't that make me a winner, too?"

"Either that or a self-deluded, overconfident little fool. Remember, I told you my plans for you before you went to bed with me, Chelsea."

"And I didn't believe you. I thought it was your wounded masculine ego talking and obviously, I didn't take you seriously. If I had—" Suddenly she felt scared and sick at the possibility that all those terrible hypothetical charges he'd invented just might be true.

No, she loved Cole. She trusted him. She had complete faith in him. He was simply feeling guilty and distraught because he thought he'd failed her by not thinking about contraception.

"I can't believe that you don't love me, Cole. Not after the things you said to me and the things we did." Her cheeks heated with color as the passionate memories swirled around her.

Her words called forth those same evocative memories for Cole as well. He felt weak with wanting, vulnerable, and his helpless response seemed a betrayal of everything he believed about himself. His so-called strength, self-control and good judgment were mere illusions when faced with his need for Chelsea.

"The things we did," he repeated. Compulsively, he attempted to wrest control of his feelings, punishing himself along with her. Because he wanted her so much that he was willing to take her to bed right now—the trip to the drugstore in Babcock be damned! He was willing to do anything to have her. It was an alarming realization, and it heightened his resolve to distance himself from her power. "What we did, what we had, was great sex, Chelsea."

"It was so much more than that, and you know it, Cole," she said quietly.

He clenched his fists to keep from grabbing her. If he touched her, he knew they would both be lost. Chelsea wouldn't stop him, and dammit, he couldn't stop himself!

"I know that you're trying to parlay great sex into true love because you can't accept it any other way. But I've outgrown that particular delusion. I don't have to be in love to enjoy myself in bed."

"You're telling me that today and last night was just a sham?" It was getting harder and harder for her to convince herself that Cole didn't mean what he was saying. He sounded so hard, so adamant. "D-did you just use me sexually to satisfy your—your lust? For revenge?"

She stared at him, trembling, but the man standing before her appeared cool and calm. "Were you lying when you said that you loved me?" she asked, her voice a pain-filled whisper.

Cole ran his hand through his hair, forcing himself to maintain his image of cool control. He had been lying, hadn't he? He *must* have been lying, because four years ago he'd made a vow to never fall into that I-love-you trap again.

"You were lying," Chelsea said, swallowing convulsively. The lump in her throat was so huge, she thought it might choke her.

He gave a half-nod, curiously unable to actually speak the words aloud.

The hurt searing Chelsea couldn't be any worse than if he'd shouted at her. She felt as if her lungs had collapsed. She could hardly breathe. It couldn't be true! But even as her heart cried the denial, she knew that it was true. She was a deluded little fool, just like Cole said. And it was time to wake up from her beautiful dream and face the facts. Cole didn't love her, he'd used her. He'd been willing to play along and say the words she'd put in his mouth, but they had no meaning for him.

"Please leave me alone," she said, her voice raw and shaky.

He left the room because there was nothing else he could do. But the moment he stepped into the hall, a terrible desolation filled him. What had just happened? And how had it happened? Exactly what had he been trying to prove? And to whom? He couldn't ever remember being so confused in his entire life.

Chelsea locked the door to the bedroom, her hands shaking, her whole body churning with emotion. She felt no confusion, only heartbreak. And she decided that she was getting out of here, even if it meant walking the entire fifteen miles to the town of Babcock!

Her mind made up, she dressed carefully and sensibly for the hike, choosing jeans and a T-shirt, over which she pulled a sweatshirt and her light summer jacket. She wore two pairs of cotton socks and her comfortable, reliable sneakers.

Her suitcase would be too heavy to drag all that way, so she tucked a few essentials, including her cash and headache pills, into her purse and slung it over her shoulder.

The window was already open, and she studied the screen for several long minutes before making her first attempt to remove it. It took her a few tries and cost her two broken fingernails, but she finally managed to unlatch the screen and remove it.

The cottage was just one story high so there was less than a four foot drop to the ground. Stealthily, feeling a bit like a cat burglar, Chelsea climbed out the window and crept around to the front of the cottage where the Tremaines' private driveway doubled as the only road down the mountain.

It was more like a wide trail than a road, unpaved and filled with stones and ruts and tenacious weeds. Chelsea wondered how the big, citified limousine had managed to handle the shock of this terrain, which was far more suitable for a jeep. She had no recollection of their arrival, of course. She visualized herself as she'd been then, sound asleep, never dreaming of the heartbreak, fury and disillusionment to come.

She determinedly blinked back the swift sting of tears. She would not cry! If she were to start now, she might never stop. Besides, hiking and weeping were incompatible activities; both demanded too much energy and concentration to be simultaneously carried on. She needed to muster all her reserves for the long trek to Babcock.

Inevitably, her thoughts drifted to Cole and his reaction to her impromptu departure. How long would it take for him to find out that she'd gone and what he would do when he did? Would he follow her? Did she want him to? Chelsea gulped. She immediately stopped speculating and determinedly thrust all thoughts of Cole from her mind. She couldn't think about him anymore, not now. She didn't dare.

Cole paced the cottage, back and forth, from room to room, very much like the stock expectant-father character featured on old TV sitcoms. He felt like a rat; no, a snake, he mentally amended. That's what Chelsea had called him when he'd refused to change her tire along the interstate, and he decided that the invective was true. Both of them were.

Once again, his mind's eye compulsively called forth the image of Chelsea's face when he'd told her that he didn't love her, that he'd been using her. That what she thought was the triumph of true love was all a lie, a cruel, premeditated deception designed to hurt her. He saw it all, her wide brown eyes bleak with pain, filling with tears that she tried desperately to blink away, her lips quivering as she gulped back sobs. The pain that slashed through him was visceral in intensity.

Congratulations, scorned a harsh voice inside his head—the outraged vestiges of the long-ago Eagle Scout? *Cole Tremaine wins again. You're back in control, you've successfully executed vengeance and settled an old score.*

He'd never felt worse in his life. He strode to the small pink bedroom and rapped lightly at the door. It was locked, of course. He'd heard her lock it. "Chelsea," he said quietly.

There was no response. Cole sighed. Did he really think that there would be? He knocked again, slightly harder. "Chelsea, please open the door."

Still no answer. He glanced at his watch. She'd locked herself in less than half an hour ago; obviously, she wasn't ready to speak to him. He honestly couldn't blame her, and he owed her some privacy. He'd leave her alone a while longer and continue to stew in his self-made hell. *You deserve it,* scolded that infernal Eagle Scout, and Cole was in complete agreement. He really did.

Eventually, Chelsea became thirsty and thought longingly of the small brook that emptied into the cool, clear pool of water. She glanced at her watch and was surprised to see that more than an hour had passed since her clandestine departure. She was undoubtedly well beyond the brook now. If only she'd been able to sneak into the kitchen and get some provisions. Of course, she hadn't dared; that would have been a dead giveaway.

Her pace was steady and she'd walked for over two hours before she felt tired enough to stop. There was nowhere to sit, so she simply flopped down along the road, Indian-style. She didn't rest long. With nothing to eat or drink or nobody to talk to, simply sitting still was boring and not particularly restful either, as the painful thoughts and memories that she'd managed to keep at bay began to sneak into her unoccupied mind. Grimly, Chelsea stood and resumed walking.

Cole tried to distract himself, first with phone calls, then by reading, finally by turning on the television set and perusing its many channels. But he couldn't interest himself in anything. He was miserable, restless and on edge. Finally, he faced the facts. He wasn't going to have a moment's peace of mind until he apologized to Chelsea.

He owed it to her, he never should have said those things to her. Because they weren't true? He mentally pleaded the Fifth on that. He still wasn't ready to give her that kind of power over him. He walked to her bedroom. "Chelsea?" He knocked on the door and twisted the knob.

There was no reply and the door stayed closed. He glanced at his watch. The past two and a half hours had passed at a glacial pace for him. How could she stand to be locked in there without a single diversion? Had she fallen asleep?"

"Chelsea, are you awake?" No answer. She was sleeping peacefully while he was jumping from this activity to that in a state of high agitation. But then he was the one with the guilty conscience, he reminded himself grimly.

Poor little Chelsea, had he worn her out last night? Erotic memories of how they'd passed the night tumbled through his mind, having a powerful, physical effect on his body. And this morning . . . he remembered the breakfast she had so lovingly prepared, their sweet session of lovemaking, their walk to the pond. How much he'd enjoyed being with her, talking to her, playing with her, just being with her.

Suddenly this latest separation of theirs struck him as absurd. They were good together in every way; they should *be* together. Why couldn't he have admitted it before, without hurting Chelsea and making himself crazy? Why did he always do things his way? The hard way. The rigid way. Chelsea knew him well, she understood him and loved him in spite of his implacable foibles. She loved him. His heartbeats echoed loudly in his head.

He'd proudly boasted that she would end up begging him to take her on any terms he offered, but Cole finally made himself face reality. He would accept whatever terms she dictated, if only she forgave him. Because he was irrevocably in love with her.

It took all of his considerable willpower not to take the door off the hinges and go to her. But he restrained himself. He had no right to disturb her sleep after keeping her awake half the night—and after she'd suffered that migraine, too! Nor should he entertain any hopes of her welcoming him into her bed. He would have to earn his way back there and he was under to illusions that it was going to be easy.

His faced wracked with remorse and regret, Cole walked quietly away from the door.

Chelsea was grateful that the road was all downhill. She was able to make good time without overexerting herself. She paused and glanced up the steep trail at the distance she'd already covered. The cottage was long out of sight; surrounded by the thick mountain forest. She felt as if she were the only person left in the world.

She blinked back another rush of tears. Back in full force was that sense of loss, that soul-chilling loneliness that she'd learned to live with since her first breakup with Cole. She'd been free of that dull, insistent ache for too short a time, but even a brief respite made the return that much more painful.

Four hours. Cole stared at the clock. He'd been a saint to leave her alone for four whole hours! He switched off the baseball game which hadn't come close to engaging his interest and stalked back to the little pink bedroom. "Chelsea, let me in. I want to talk to you," he said, his voice and his knock firm.

"Honey, it's nearly six. Let's have dinner. I'll cook. Anything you want . . . except braised eels, pheasant under glass and glazed kumquats with heavy cream." He hoped to make her smile by recalling happier moments from last night.

Nothing. He pounded and pounded on the door. "Chelsea, I know you're not asleep because I've been making enough noise to wake a coma victim." His voice turned soft and coaxing. "Open the door, sweetheart. We have a lot to talk about."

When there was still no response, he knew at once what had to be done. It took just a few minutes to get his tools and remove the door from its hinges again. "Chelsea, I know you're upset but hiding in here isn't—"

He stopped in mid-sentence. She wasn't in the room. He strode through the room and flung open the bathroom door, peered inside, then whirled around and spied the screen on the floor beside the open window.

She wasn't hiding in the room, she hadn't been sleeping in it. She'd climbed out the window and left him! Cole blanched. When? Four hours ago?

He knew she had to be walking but she might have gone as far as eight or nine miles if she'd kept up a steady pace. She would be coming to the end of the Tremaines' private access road and nearing the main road into Babcock, which, except for the final mile leading into town, wasn't much of a road at all, just a gravelly old country lane barely wide enough for two cars.

Chelsea was gone! His breathing seemed to stop. The pain that shot through him was so fierce, so crippling that for a moment he couldn't move or utter a sound. He'd driven her away and now he was alone again, free to live his life without her. And she was alone, too, all alone on a remote mountain trail, miles from any help should she need it. And within a very few hours, it would be dark!

As he dashed out of the room, he happened to catch a glimpse of himself in the pink-framed mirror on the wall. He looked exactly the way she had four hours earlier, when he'd said all those things that had caused her to run away from him. Desolate. Devastated. So very lost and alone.

* * *

Because there were no other sounds but those of the forest, a noise from the man-made world of civilization was instantly decipherable and jarring. Chelsea's first thought was that the faint sound of a car engine was out of place and out of time here. Then her breath caught in her throat.

A car! She was certain Cole was coming after her in the limousine. The sounds were coming from the direction of the cottage. She glanced at her watch. She'd been gone over four hours and she had no idea how far she'd come or how far she had to go. She did know one thing, though. She was not about to get into the car with Cole Tremaine.

Chelsea ran from the road toward a thick grove of trees several yards away. There were clumps of bushes and tall weeds, too. If she were to lie down flat, she would be invisible from the road. Gingerly, she stretched out on her stomach, making a face as she felt the damp, cool ground beneath her.

There wasn't a sign of Chelsea anywhere. Cole braked the limousine to a halt and climbed out, his gaze sweeping the narrow road and surrounding panorama. There were trees and greenery on all sides, as far as the eye could see. And she was nowhere in sight.

His heart thundering, the blood roaring in his ears, Cole cupped his hands to his mouth and shouted her name. The sound echoed faintly in the stillness, but there was no response. He called her again. Still nothing.

He sounded far away, but she heard him. Carefully, Chelsea lifted her head a little. He was nowhere in sight, and neither was the car. She guessed he was a considerable distance up the mountain, but she didn't want to risk detection, so she lay back down again.

"Chelsea, if you can hear me, for heaven's sake answer me!" Cole's voice was hoarse from yelling. Frustration mixed with an increasing panic. Where was she? Suppose she'd injured herself somehow and was lying unconscious and helpless, unable to hear him or too weak to respond. And she could be pregnant!

Cole jumped back into the car and headed down the mountain another few miles, then got out and began to call her again.

"Chelsea, please! Let me know where you are!"

Oh, right! Chelsea growled under her breath. He was closer, still out of sight, but sounding nearer. *I'll just stand up and holler: here I am, come and get me. I'm dying to experience a little more of the torture you dish out.*

"Chelsea, if you're hurt, I want to help you."

So that was why he'd come hotfooting after her. A cynical smile twisted Chelsea's lips. He was afraid she'd get hurt out here in the wilds and he didn't want that on his conscience. He didn't care that he had devastated her emotionally, he'd enjoyed that, but a physical injury, such as a sprained ankle, might make him appear unchivalrous. Perhaps it might also make him a target of her vengeance—loving, litigious parents. They could file a personal injury claim against him on her behalf. As a meticulous attorney, Cole would undoubtedly be aware of that angle.

Cole paced the road like a caged animal, tension spiraling tautly through him. If only he could go back four hours ago in time and wipe out the things he'd said. If only he could go back four years ago, to the day of their engagement party, when she'd pleaded with him for more time before setting their wedding date.

This time he'd listen seriously to everything she had to say, to all her uncertainties and doubts and fear of marriage and divorce. He would be so understanding and patient that she would tell him all about her embittered, embattled parents and their vindictive one-upsmanship games during her childhood, of the pain and misery she'd felt as a pawn in those financial and emotional parental wars. And he would give her the time she needed, that they both needed, to build a strong, lasting relationship.

He loved her; he'd never stopped loving her. But then, as now, he'd been too proud, too rigid, too controlling and stubborn to let her know how deeply he cared.

"Chelsea! I love you!" He shouted it so loud that his throat felt raw and sore. "Baby, please come back to me!"

From her hiding place, Chelsea listened to his impassioned declaration with a sardonic grimace. He loved her. Ha! Where had she heard that one before? Did he really think she was stupid enough to believe him *again*?

"Chelsea, I'm sorry for hurting you. I know I don't deserve it, but please give me a chance to make it up to you. I love you, darling."

Chelsea lay rigid and tense, not moving a muscle. She swallowed the lump that had suddenly lodged in her throat. She was horrified by how very much she wanted to believe him! Her gullibility, her vulnerability where this man was concerned simultaneously alarmed her and enraged her. She was as susceptible to Cole Tremaine as a person with an immune deficiency was to germs!

"Chelsea, I know it must be hard for you to listen to me and believe what I'm saying." Cole's voice, loud and clear and plaintive echoed over the mountainside. "But, sweetheart, it's the truth. I love you. Trust your instincts and come to me, darling."

Chelsea shook her head with disbelief. She'd believed that he loved her when he had told her so last night, their bodies still joined, moist and warm from the intimacy they had shared. She'd trusted her instincts then, only to have the words thrown back in her face in the cool light of day. She had loved him and he'd hurt her more than she'd ever imagined she could hurt. Her feminine intuition was a joke!

She lay silent and still, listening and waiting. Finally he stopped calling. But it wasn't over, she still wasn't safe. He was back in the car and she froze as she heard it coming nearer.

Nine

Chelsea held her breath as the car inched along the road at an agonizingly slow pace. Obviously, Cole was scanning the area as he drove. She closed her eyes and kept her face buried in the cradle of her arms as the car approached. She was only a few yards from the road; if she were to stand up, or even sit up, she'd make a noise and he would find her easily.

She couldn't let him find her; she couldn't let him take her back to the cottage. She simply couldn't stand it.

Chelsea let out a long, shaky breath when she heard the car pass, but she didn't move. About half a mile down the road, Cole stopped the car, got out, and began to call her again.

"Chelsea, it's going to be dark in a couple of hours. The temperature will drop. Please, sweetheart, don't risk it. There are no lights out here, it gets so dark that you can barely see your hand in front of your face. And it gets cold, too. You won't want to be out here alone, Chelsea!"

She shivered. He wasn't painting a very appealing portrait of the mountains by night. She'd never been particularly enamored of the dark, and her clothes were already damp from lying on the ground. But she still didn't reveal her hiding place. Anything was preferable to being with that liar, that cold-blooded heartbreaker, she assured herself. Even lying on the damp ground all through the dark, cold night.

After a few more tries, Cole gave up, got back in the car, and continued his trek down the mountains. Chelsea sat up, frowning, wondering what to do. The car was out of sight now; should she resume walking? Or would that be an invitation to be found?

She glanced nervously at her watch. It was already going on seven. Although the summer days were longest in June, she couldn't expect the daylight hours to last much beyond nine o'clock, and maybe not even that late. Her stomach growled, reminding her that she was hungry. And, ominously, a nasty little dart of pain arrowed through her head.

Not another migraine! She'd never had them just one day apart. Usually, there was a number of weeks, even months, between attacks. But these past two days were like nothing she had ever experienced before, Chelsea acknowledged grimly. Did she dare take her pills on an empty stomach? What if they made her sleepy?

Remembering the potent effect they'd had yesterday, she decided not to risk it, but the little flash of pain did help her reach a decision. She had to get out of here and soon. She stood up and made her way back to the trail-like road.

She had one near miss, nearly an hour later. She heard the car again, coming toward her. Cole must have decided to retrace his path and was headed back up the mountains. Chelsea ran from the road and huddled behind the trunk of a massive oak where she waited and listened to Cole call her, plead with her, try to scare her.

He'd added some new dangers to his list, along with the darkness and the cold. "Chelsea, there are wild animals out here. Bears, foxes and Lord only knows what else. There are snakes. And—poison ivy."

She quickly glanced down at her hands, as if expecting to see a nasty rash covering them. She fervently hoped that she hadn't thrown herself down into a bed of poison ivy while hiding from him. Still, she remained where she was, resisting any temptation to go to him. Nothing nature tossed her way could hurt her as much as the man she had loved and trusted.

Cole continued his search and Chelsea continued her escape. She was trudging along the interminable road when the sound of a car once again shattered the silence of the mountainside. This time she had no time to hide; the car was traveling fast, too fast for the twisting, unpaved road.

When the beat-up green Chevy screeched to a halt a few feet ahead of her, she was torn between relief, astonishment and dread.

"Hey, Chelsea!" Miles Rodgers yelled out the front window from the passenger side. "Want a ride?"

"I'm going into Babcock," she said warily, walking up to the car. "Is it far?"

Kieran Kaufman leaned out the window of the driver's side. "There's nothing in that hick town, just a Mom-and-Pop grocery and a drugstore. Want us to take you back to D.C.?"

"Not if you're still set on making some stupid videotape," she said severely. "I'd rather walk to Babcock and spend the night in the bus station than do that."

"There is no bus station in Babcock," said Kaufman. "Anyway, we dumped the video idea. Strickland's already released a boring, bland statement about the wedding being called off for mutual, personal reasons. But there's a hot new rumor afloat that Seth is going to marry someone else any day now. Rumor has it he allegedly fell in love with this new woman after he met you and that's the real reason why the wedding was canceled. If it's true, you're old news, Chelsea."

"Nothing could make me happier," she breathed. She wondered if Seth had actually managed to come up with a replacement candidate or was floating the rumor as a face-saving device. She didn't really care either way.

"So how come you ran out on your boyfriend, Chelsea?" Miles Rodgers asked, eyeing her curiously. "Not Strickland, but Cole Tremaine. We saw the poor guy less than half an hour ago, yelling his lungs out for you. He was in a real panic, half out of his mind with worry. I felt real sorry for him."

"You saw Cole?" cried Chelsea. "You talked to him?"

"He flagged us down and asked if we'd seen a young red-haired woman along the road to Babcock," Kaufman explained. "He didn't recognize us. But we knew him, of course. We'd traced the license plate number of the limo that took you off to Tremaine Incorporated. Once we had the Tremaine connection, we tapped into sources who told us that you and Cole had once been nearly engaged. And that you dumped him—or maybe he dumped you. Sometimes our sources aren't too clear on the facts."

"The understatement of the year," Chelsea murmured. "What are you two doing out here, anyway? Did you come looking for me?"

"Sure," Miles admitted easily. "After Kieran and I escaped from those agency mutants we decided to find you and Cole Tremaine and do a human interest story."

"We found out about the Tremaine family's place in the Catoctins," Kieran interjected. "A cozy little love nest for you and Cole to run to, huh, Chelse?"

Chelsea was awed in spite of herself. "How did you get all that information?"

"We have our ways and means," Kaufman said cheerfully. "I'm not going to tell you what they are because you'd just get offended and call us a pair of slime-buckets."

"Anyway, we still need a legitimate scoop and until we find out the name of Strickland's new bride, all our hopes are on you, Chelsea," added Miles. "We're planning a serious, classy story, something about the rocky course of true love, yours and Tremaine's. How it's lasted through your broken engagement and the Seth Strickland fiasco and even this latest fight of yours, with you running away and him chasing you through the mountains. What do you think?"

Chelsea's eyes filled with tears. "You'll have to find some other story, Miles. Cole doesn't love me." To her horror, she began to cry.

Kaufman and Rodgers exchanged glances.

"Of course he does," Rodgers said solicitously. "We saw him, remember? Only a man who's really in love gets that demented over a woman."

"We'll be glad to take you back to him," put in Kaufman. "If you'll direct us to his place, that remote hideaway for a flight-from-the-altar rendezvous. Got lots of film, Miles?"

"Affirmative," Miles reported.

"I can't go back to Cole. Not ever. He doesn't love me, he was only pretending. He told me so." Chelsea voice broke on a sob. "Will you take me home? Back to my apartment in Washington? Please!"

"You're a lot of trouble, you know," Kaufman said sourly. "I think I prefer writing about dead rock stars who appear in bowling alleys and space aliens who flush themselves down the drain and terrorize the city's sewers, to your botched romances."

"Of course we'll drive you home, Chelsea," Miles Rodgers soothed. "I'll be glad to get back to the city, anyway. I hate all this fresh air. My lungs can't handle it."

Chelsea climbed into the backseat of the car. She took her headache pills with a swig of Miles's orange soda. Her migraine was arrested, but not her tears. She cried the whole way to Interstate 70, she cried when they stopped for sandwiches at a rest area, she cried between bites of ham and cheese and gulps of lemonade. She cried an ocean of tears, yet more continued to fall. She couldn't seem to stop them.

"Kid, we're getting waterlogged," Kieran Kaufman complained at last. "If you're this broken up over the guy, why'd you leave him in the first place? And I won't even bother to ask how you happened to get yourself engaged to Seth Strickland when you're nuts about another man. There are some unsolved mysteries that defy human explanation and understanding."

"I'm too upset to talk about it," Chelsea said with a sad little sniff. "And even if I wanted to talk, you two are probably the last people on earth I'd confide in. I wouldn't want my private life splashed across the disgusting *Globe Star Probe* accompanied by a ghoulish headline and composite pictures."

"We're not going to write your story," Miles assured her. "It's not heartwarming enough or gross enough or even interesting enough for our readers as it now stands."

"We'd have to add something," agreed Kieran. "Maybe a supernatural angle? Something along the lines of *Dead Mom Returns from Grave to Scold Errant Son for Breaking Lover's Heart*." He glanced back at Chelsea. "Like that? If we could get a picture of Marnie Tremaine and superimpose it on a gravestone, preferably hers, it might fly."

"How did you know Cole's mother's name?" Chelsea asked. She was stunned by the extent of his knowledge. "How did you know that she's dead?"

Kaufman shrugged. "I'm a good reporter, even if I do work for a gag rag. Yesterday I did a lot of digging into the Tremaine family history. Little Cole was not quite eight when his mother died in that car accident. You should've taken that fact into consideration before you got mixed up with him, Chelsea. Getting involved with someone who's lost a parent as a child is risky. And when it's the parent of the opposite sex, it's double jeopardy."

"Do you moonlight as a psychiatrist when you're not cooking up stories for the *Probe*?" Chelsea asked caustically.

"I'm speaking from personal experience, babe. The love of my life lost her daddy at age eleven. She had an abandonment complex that just wouldn't quit. She associated loving a man with being abandoned, so when she grew up, she *expected* the man she loved to leave her. She kept setting it up, she drove me away to make it fit her expectations. My shrink explained it all to me when she and I broke up for the final time."

He shook his head, and laughed a little. "Yeah, I actually consulted a shrink, I felt so terrible about losing her. That was back in the days before I became shallow and unfeeling. Believe me, it's easier to live your life not caring about anyone or anything. I highly recommend it."

Chelsea sat very still. Never had she thought that anything or anyone with even a remote connection to the *Globe Star Probe* would have some relevance to her life. But Kieran Kaufman's remarks about abandonment, about setting up a loved one to leave were right on target. Hadn't Cole done that to her today?

Then again, maybe he hadn't, she decided sadly. Maybe she was looking for reasons to keep herself from accepting the actual truth: that Cole simply didn't love her.

"Of course, you children of divorce are no prizes either, Chelsea," Kaufman continued in the same cool impassive manner. "Those feelings of powerlessness and betrayal that kids feel when their parents break up leave scars. But when the conflict continues after the divorce, the scars never have a chance to heal. Tremaine should've had his head examined before taking up with a woman whose parents have committed more kidnappings than a Beirut street gang. No wonder the two of you have had such a tumultuous romantic history. As a couple, you're a disaster zone."

"Kaufman, shut up," Chelsea ordered, but her expression was thoughtful and she was no longer crying. She was thinking about Cole calling to her on the mountain, of the anxiety and panic in his voice. About abandonment, powerlessness and betrayal, about haunting childhood memories, his and hers, that impacted on the present.

"Could we pull off at the next exit and find a phone?" she asked. "I think I ought to let Cole know that I'm all right, that I haven't been eaten by a bear on the mountain or succumbed to a fatal case of poison ivy."

"Good idea," approved Miles.

"Just don't expect me to drive you all the way back to that godforsaken mountain," growled Kaufman. "If you want to make up with him, do it in the city on your own time and your own gas."

"I'm not thinking about making up, I just don't think Cole deserves to spend the whole night wondering where I am." She ignored Kaufman's impatient sigh of exasperation.

They found a pay phone outside a convenience store and truck stop near an exit off the interstate. There, Chelsea remembered she didn't know the phone number at the cottage. Her only recourse was to call Stefanie and report she was on her way home. If Cole happened to call her sister, she could give him the news.

"Chelsea, where are you?" Stefanie exclaimed before Chelsea could tell her. "Cole has called three times asking if I'd heard from you. He's crazy with worry. His voice is so hoarse from yelling on that mountain that he can hardly talk."

Chelsea assured her sister that she was safe and on her way home.

"Oh, I knew you were okay. I told Cole that my big sister can take care of herself," Stefanie said blithely. She cleared her throat. "Chelse, I—uh—have something to tell you." This time the breeziness was noticeably absent from her tone. "I thought I'd wait till I saw you, but maybe you'd better know now."

Over the line, Chelsea heard her sister take a deep, audible breath. "What is it, Steffie?" she asked, suddenly worried. Stefanie could be alarmingly unpredictable at times.

"I'm getting married, Chelsea," Stefanie said in a rush. "Soon. Within a couple of days. Chelsea, I'm marrying Seth Strickland."

Chelsea opened her mouth to speak. Not a single sound came out.

"I talked to him the day the wedding was canceled and I was, well, commiserating with him," Stefanie hurried to fill the silence. "You know, it was terribly humiliating for him and his family, Chelse. I felt sorry for Seth and told him if there was anything I could do to help, he should let me know."

"So he asked you to marry him?" Chelsea's voice was back, though rather high and squeaky. "You can't do it, Stefanie! You don't love him and he doesn't love you. You'll—"

"Well, of course not," Stefanie interrupted coolly. "Unlike you, I'm not looking for love in marriage, Chelsea. You may believe in it, but I don't. What I believe in is the mutually advantageous contract Seth and I have drawn up and signed. Something as illusionary and subjective as *love* has no place in that."

"Stefanie, this is insane! I can understand Seth wanting to salvage his pride, and marrying you right away might be one way to do it, but there is no way this cold-blooded arrangement could benefit you in any way."

"Chelsea, it's going to benefit me in every way! As soon as I signed the contract a cash settlement of a quarter-million dollars was deposited in my bank account. If I worked my whole life at my dull government job, I'd never see that kind of money. Chelsea, I'm rich! Just like I've always dreamed!"

Chelsea's thoughts flashed back to their younger days, to Halloween when Stefanie had eschewed the traditional witch or cheerleader costumes of the other little girls because she wanted to dress up as "a rich person." They gave her a big purse and lots of junk jewelry from the five-and-ten, and everybody thought she was pretending to be "a grown-up lady."

"No," little Stefanie had said, her big dark eyes serious. "I'm a rich person." Every single Halloween.

"Oh, Stefanie!" Chelsea moaned into the phone.

"Chelsea, I'm happy!" Stefanie insisted. "For the first time in my life I'm really happy! I hated growing up poor with Mother, wearing your hand-me-downs, watching every penny. And I hated having to be ingratiating with Daddy when we really needed something because he was the one with the cash. It was deadly."

"Of course it was, Stefanie, but that's all in the past. You worked your way through college so you could have a good job and be independent. And you did. You are!"

"I've got my degree and now I'm stuck in a boring job that pays a living wage but will never make me rich. What I'd really like to be is a photographer but I'm not good enough to support myself as one. My life was in a dismal rut until you called off your wedding and Seth asked me to be a Strickland."

Stefanie's voice turned rapturous. "Me, a Strickland! A member of the First Family! Just think of all the new clothes and the parties and the travel! I've never been anywhere, Chelsea. Now Seth wants us to make goodwill trips all over the world! And I bet some publishing house will offer me a contract for a book of my photographs, too, something that would never happen without the Strickland name. *My* new name—Stefanie Strickland. It even sounds right and rich, doesn't it, Chelsea?"

Where were the words of big sisterly advice she should be giving Stefanie to turn her around? Chelsea wondered as she listened to her younger sister prattle on. She was so shocked by the unexpected news that all she could manage was a worn-out cliché. "If you marry for money, you'll end up earning it the hard way, Stefanie."

"Marrying for money is more sound than marrying for love," Stefanie shot back. "Look at Mom and Dad. They claimed they were madly in love when they got married. Compare that catastrophe to their second marriages, which have lasted. Mom married Jack for economic security, and Dad married Linda because he was tired of playing the field and needed the convenience of a wife. Marrying for love equals marrying for misery. I never want to lose my head or my heart over anyone, Chelsea."

Chelsea tried again and again to dissuade her, but Stefanie rebutted her at every turn, until Kieran Kaufman leaned on the horn of the old green Chevy to summon her to the car.

"We're not spending the night here," Kaufman snapped. "Get in and let's go."

Feeling shell-shocked, Chelsea climbed back into the car. "I know who Seth Strickland's new bride is," she said, aware that she was perpetrating a fiendish deed. But desperate situations sometimes required unorthodox tactics. "If I tell you her name and address, will you promise to go directly to her apartment and harass her until she grants you an interview?"

"Honey, you can count on it!" exclaimed Miles.

She gave them Stefanie's name and address. "I'm hoping that after meeting you two, Stefanie will realize there's a dark side to fame," Chelsea said grimly. "I'm counting on you guys to trick her into saying something so outrageous and indiscreet that the Stricklands will decide that this marriage isn't a good idea, after all. If anyone can do it, you two can."

"We appreciate your faith in us, but this interview is going to be done strictly with taste and class," retorted Kieran. "This is our big shot at a network exclusive, remember? Our chance to leave the pits for the pros. We're not going to blow it and we'll make sure your little sister doesn't, either."

Chelsea didn't give up hope. Taste and class were hardly the hallmark of the *Globe Star Probe* and Kaufman and Rodgers were the tabloid's top reporters. Once they heard Stefanie's rhapsody to riches, everything would fall into place. Outrageous and indiscreet would hardly describe the interview that would, hopefully, put an end to Stefanie's disastrous plans.

Kaufman and Rodgers dropped Chelsea off in the parking lot of her apartment building and sped off into the night, not bothering to see her to her door. They were on their way to nab an exclusive scoop and she was yesterday's news.

As she made her way to the door of the building, she spied her little Honda parked in its usual spot, its flat tire replaced with a good one, and looking none the worse for its roadside abandonment. Once again, she felt the sting of tears in her eyes. Cole had done as he'd promised and had returned her car. That didn't surprise her; he was dependable, reliable, a man of action, a man of his word.

Except when it came to loving. She determinedly blinked back her tears. She was too weary to cry anymore; she had to pull herself together and stop weeping over what she couldn't have. Cole Tremaine.

Fumbling through her purse, she found her keys and let herself into her dark apartment. Her precipitous early morning flight had precluded any thoughts of leaving on a light for her return. As her eyes adjusted to the blackness, she tentatively made her way to the nearest lamp, which sat on an end table beside the couch.

Before she reached it, she heard a small click, then blinked as light illuminated the room. Chelsea started violently and uttered a strangled gasp. Cole was sitting on the couch, looking tired and disheveled.

"What are you doing here? How did you get in? How did you get here before me?" she asked in one breath, then had to pause to exhale.

"As soon as Stefanie told me you were on your way back here, I arranged for the company plane to meet me at the county airport several miles east of Babcock," said Cole. His voice was strained and sounded rasping and hoarse. "It's a short flight," he added, shrugging. "I had time to go over to Stefanie's, borrow the key you gave her and let myself in. I've been waiting for you. She told me you'd called her, but I had to see you."

"Why?" she asked coldly. It was too much for her to cope with, having him here after she'd spent hours mourning the loss of him. She was heartily sick of the roller-coaster ups and downs of the past days. Stefanie's words suddenly echoed in her ears. *I never want to lose my head or my heart over anyone.* Maybe her little sister had the right idea, after all.

"Earlier today, down by the pond, you told me to never let you go again," Cole said quietly.

Chelsea's cheeks flushed a warm pink. "We both said a lot of things we didn't mean in the past day or so."

"You didn't. You said you love me and you do. You asked me to never let you go again and I'm not going to. We're going to have another whirlwind courtship, Chelsea. And this one is going to end in marriage."

"How?" she snapped. "You're never going to propose to me again, remember? And I certainly won't propose to you. I don't even want to hear the word *marriage*. It's been responsible for this whole mess! You, me, Seth, Stefanie—"

She paused in mid-tirade. Now that Cole was here, it was impossible to keep the troubling news to herself. "Stefanie is going to marry Seth Strickland—because he's rich and he's the President's son. They signed some sort of premarital contract and I'm worried sick about her."

A thoughtful smile curved Cole's lips. "So that's why Stefanie's been so helpful and encouraging to me...she wants to be certain that you're completely out of the picture so she can consolidate her gains with Strickland. Looks like the little gold digger has struck the mother lode. She must be absolutely ecstatic."

"That's a terrible thing to say!" Chelsea hissed, glaring at him. "I thought you liked Stefanie."

"I do. I always have. But that doesn't prevent me from seeing exactly what she's about. Remember how Stefanie was always pestering me to fix her up with Tyler or Nathaniel four years ago?"

"She thought it would be fun to double date with you and me," Chelsea said coolly. "Your brothers both thought she was too young for them and didn't take her out."

"But not because she was too young. That was merely a polite ruse. Neither of my brothers would've had any qualms about dating a sexy, sultry little blonde like Stefanie then or now—except that she fairly radiated fortune-hunter vibes. When it came to money, she was like a Geiger counter near a uranium mine. My brothers and I learned very early how to spot women who were more interested in our bank statements than ourselves."

"I will not stand here and listen to a two-faced, back-stabbing hypocrite like yourself malign my little sister. I want you to leave my apartment right now, Cole Tremaine."

Cole didn't budge. "I wasn't maligning Stefanie. I just didn't want you worrying about her. That little lady can take care of herself."

"Out!" Chelsea was outraged.

"Before I leave, will you tell me who brought you back here tonight? And—if you heard me calling you on the mountain this afternoon?"

"I heard you. And I was very careful to stay hidden. Sometime after seven o'clock, Kaufman and Rodgers from the *Globe Star Probe* drove by an offered me a ride back to the city. I took it. Now go."

"Not before I tell you that I meant every word I said out on the mountain today, Chelsea. I'm sorry I hurt you and I want another chance to make it up to you. I love you and have never stopped loving you."

She faced him with a bitter weariness. "Cole, four years ago you told me you loved me but when I wouldn't marry you on the date you demanded, you left me. For four whole years I never heard a word from you, although you were busy behind the scenes sabotaging *Capitol Scene* to punish me. When we were in the mountains, I let myself believe that you really did love me. After all, you looked me in the eyes and said that obligatory catchphrase, 'I love you.' And then you took it all back. Now you're telling me you love me again."

She flopped down on the armchair opposite the sofa and stared at the floor. "I don't want to hear it, Cole. I don't believe you. It's all over between us and it's a good thing because as a couple we're a—a disaster zone." Good Lord, she was quoting Kieran Kaufman. What was next? A weekly subscription to the *Probe*?

She waited, tense and expectant, for his response. She knew very well that when Cole Tremaine was intent upon a course of action he was like a guided missile, relentlessly advancing toward its target. He didn't take kindly to anything or anyone who attempted to divert him. She saw his expression tighten and wondered if he was going to lose his temper.

"We haven't had it easy," he said with careful, calm control. "Some couples meet, fall in love and get married without any problems, conflicts and crises. We've followed a different course, but—"

"The rocky course of true love," Chelsea cut in mockingly. "Kaufman and Rodgers thought about doing a story on us, but ultimately deemed our tale unfit for *Globe Star Probe* consumption."

"I'm grateful for that, at least." He moved to stand above her chair, fastening his hand around the nape of her neck. "I know tonight isn't a good time to talk about our future, Chelsea. You're tired and hurt and not up to another emotional confrontation. But I want you to know how sorry I am about today. When I found out that you'd left me, that you preferred to risk being alone in the mountains at night rather than come back to me..."

He paused and took a deep breath. Chelsea glanced up at him warily. His face was bleak. "It was all my fault and I have to pay the penalty for my own stupidity. But that doesn't mean I'm giving up, Chelsea. Because I know that beneath all your anger and hurt, you love me. And when you decide I've been punished enough, you'll admit it to yourself. Then we can finally be together."

His fingers were caressing her nape in slow, erotic strokes and something very primitive and very feminine rippled through her. She quickly rose to her feet and pulled away from him. "It's not going to work, Cole. This time you aren't going to cloud my judgment with sex."

"I wasn't trying to." A slow smile crossed his face. "I hadn't given a thought to turning on the sexual heat, but you responded to me anyway. That's the way it is between us, Chelsea. All I have to do is touch you and you feel aroused. And your touch has the identical effect on me."

"I'm not going to go to bed with you, Cole!" she flared. "Sex is another area I've decided to steer clear of. It's currently tied with marriage at the top of my troubles-to-avoid list."

"I could take you in my arms and we'd be in bed within ten minutes flat." The rawness of his voice enhanced his potent sexuality.

Chelsea fought the instinctive feminine excitement stirred by his demands. It was imperative that she prove to him that she was not his to command, not sexually or emotionally or any other way. That there were times when she was in control and he couldn't take over and take charge.

She sensed the intensity of his need to do exactly that. And the burgeoning surge of his powerful body provided visible evidence of his desire for her. His deep blue eyes were burning with masculine intent—and frustration. Chelsea braced herself, certain he would try to exert his mastery over her to make her change her mind.

"You want me, Chelsea." Cole cupped her shoulder with his big hands and began to draw her slowly, inexorably to him. "Don't fight me, darling, don't fight yourself. We're so good together. We belong together, my baby."

She wouldn't succumb to him, Chelsea promised herself. She wouldn't give him the surrender he demanded. Not again. *She couldn't!*

"I don't want this, Cole," she said in a voice that was too shaky and too husky for a man bent on seduction to take seriously. "I want you to go home. I need to be alone tonight."

Something flickered in Cole's eyes and he dropped his hands. The onslaught came to an immediate halt. He shrugged dispiritedly. "I've done some stupid things in the past, but that doesn't mean that I *am* stupid. It's taken long enough, but I've finally begun to learn from my mistakes. I'm not going to seduce you tonight, Chelsea, as much as I might want to."

He leaned down and gave her a quick, chaste kiss on her forehead. "There's just one other thing, Chelsea. 'I love you' isn't an obligatory catchphrase and never has been. I've been the deluded fool, thinking I could separate love from sex, denying my true feelings for you to myself. I do love you, Chelsea, and I'll back the words with the actions to prove it to you. I won't lose you again."

He turned and quickly left the apartment.

For several long moments after he'd gone, Chelsea stood staring at the door in bemusement. She couldn't quite figure it out. She had told him to go, and though he didn't want to, he'd left. She had said she didn't want him to make love to her, and though he was hungry for her and *knew she wanted him, too,* he'd acquiesced to her wishes.

It didn't fit at all what she knew of Cole Tremaine, the dominating, aggressive, winner-take-all man. Was he playing a dangerous new game of manipulation?

Maybe he didn't want her that much, after all. Chelsea tried to ignore the shaft of pain that accompanied that humbling conjecture.

It was difficult for her to give much credibility to the third possibility: that he was willing to give up complete control in their relationship and take her needs and opinions into consideration. That he had ceded power to her even though it meant giving up the certain victory of his power over her. That he was willing to prove that he loved her with his actions speaking more effectively than words.

Ten

"Breakfast is ready."

Chelsea jerked awake at the sound and her wide, startled eyes instantly focused upon Cole, standing at the foot of her bed. He was wearing his executive intimidation clothes, a charcoal-gray suit, white shirt and silk rep tie. He looked dignified, powerful and ridiculously out of place in her feminine violet and cream bedroom.

"Fresh from McDonald's drive-thru window," Cole said dryly, offering her a wrapped sausage biscuit and plastic container of juice. "I wanted to return the favor and serve you a delicious, homecooked breakfast in bed but your refrigerator was practically bare and I didn't have time for a grocery run."

"How did you get in?" Chelsea croaked in a voice still thick with sleep.

Her eyes darted to the bedside clock. It was a little past nine. She drew the sheet up to her chin, excruciatingly aware that she was naked. After Cole's early morning departure, she'd been so mentally and physically exhausted that she'd stripped off her clothes and fallen into bed and a deep and, mercifully, dreamless sleep. She had not expected to awaken to Cole Tremaine in her bedroom.

Cole set the food on the nightstand. "I kept the key I borrowed from Stefanie." His eyes swept over her assessingly. "You still look tired. Why don't you eat your breakfast while it's hot and then go back to sleep?"

She shook her head. "I'm going into work today. As soon as I shower and dress."

"I guess you'd turn down my offer to help you with that, were I to make one?" he drawled. He fixed his gaze on the sheet and her shapely outline beneath it.

Chelsea felt a slow blush suffuse her entire body. Did he know she was nude? "Yes, I would," she retorted, a little too breathlessly for her liking.

"I thought you might. If you'll tell me where your robe is, I'll fetch it for you." His eyes were hooded, his expression totally enigmatic. "You'll need it—it's hard to hold up that sheet and eat at the same time."

Her blush deepened. He did know! There was another awkward moment when he handed her the bright, floral-print muumuu that she used as a summer robe.

"My father brought you this from one of his trips to Hawaii," Cole said, remembering it. "And you kept it all this time."

"It's very comfortable, very practical," she said stiffly. "If you'll excuse me, I—I'll put it on." Her face was hot. After all the intimacies she and Cole had shared, her demand for such propriety seemed prim and ridiculous. But to casually dress in front of him at this particular point in time seemed an impossible alternative.

Cole's lips twitched and he dutifully turned his back to her. "Do I have to promise not to turn around?"

"Yes!" She yanked the muumuu over her head and struggled to smooth it over her hips and legs. She completed the task not a moment too soon, because Cole whirled around, his blue eyes gleaming.

She was unsettled and unnerved by his presence, he noted with satisfaction. A good sign, a very good sign. Last night, she'd been depleted and drained to the point of being unreachable, and that had alarmed him far more than having to cope with her hostility. Now she was intensely aware of him and the tension crackling between them was as sharp as ever.

He watched her swing her legs over the side of the bed, saw her eyeing the breakfast on the nightstand. He quickly unwrapped the sausage biscuit and handed it to her.

Chelsea considered it hungrily, suddenly reminded that she hadn't eaten in hours. Those few tearful bites of the sandwich she'd had on the road had been her last meal. As Cole opened the container of juice, she began to eat.

The doorbell rang. "I'll get that. You go on eating," Cole ordered and left the room. A few minutes later, he was back with four long white boxes, tied with starched ribbons. "For you," he said, laying them on the bed.

"Flowers." Chelsea's eyes met his. "Roses. From you." She knew it before she opened the first box.

"Am I that predictable?" Cole complained mildly.

"You always used to send me roses from this florist." She untied the ribbon, opened the box and looked at the dozen long-stemmed red roses nestled within. There was a small sealed envelope and she opened it with a sense of nervous anticipation. *I love you,* was written on the card in Cole's handwriting.

"Ah, the obligatory catchphrase, a guaranteed ticket into bed." She'd intended to sound breezily cool and was appalled that her voice trembled as she spoke. Even to her own ears, she sounded hurt and vulnerable instead.

"No." Cole took her hand and lifted it to his mouth, pressing his lips against her palm. "No, baby, it's not."

She felt his tongue against the sensitive skin and a current of hot sparks swirled in her middle, growing sharper and lower as his lips brushed her fingertips.

With a shuddery little sigh, she withdrew her hand and opened the next three boxes. The contents of each were identical to the first. The roses, the handwritten card.

"Four. One for every year we've been apart," she murmured, wishing she weren't quite so attuned to him. He nodded his head in affirmation. "Thank you, Cole. They're beautiful. I'll be able to put at least one dozen in the vase you bought me especially for roses four years ago."

"You still have the vase?"

"One tends to hang on to a Steuben vase when it comes her way," Chelsea said dryly. "Of course I still have it. I treasure it."

He looked pleased. "Good. I'll arrange to have three more sent over today."

"No, don't! I—don't want you showering me with expensive presents, Cole. I don't want the obligations they entail."

"There are no strings attached, Chelsea. I want to give you things. This is a courtship, remember?"

"Cole, last night I—"

"It's a paradoxical whirlwind courtship though," Cole cut in quickly. "Because I'm going to give you all the time and space you want and need to be sure of me, Chelsea. This time you're the one calling all the shots."

"Cole, I said last night that it was over and—"

"Except that," Cole interrupted again. "That's the one shot I won't let you call, Chelsea. It'll never be over between us."

"Well, my reign of power didn't last very long," Chelsea said, her dark eyes lighting with humor in spite of herself. "All of five seconds. Looks like you're back in command."

"I keep remembering how you clung to me and told me never, never to let you go again," he said softly and his eyes blazed with intensity. "I won't, Chelsea. Deal with it."

Chelsea gritted her teeth at his arrogant assumption that she was his for the taking—and keeping. She was about to tell him exactly what *he* could deal with when Cole pulled her into his arms and covered her mouth with his.

Her self-control, never in peak form when she was in Cole's arms, failed her completely. His mouth was hot and hungry on hers and he penetrated the moist softness of her mouth with his tongue, deepening the kiss with shattering intimacy. She moaned and slid her arms around his neck, fitting herself to him, as she trembled and shivered with desire.

She felt the burning masculine heat of his body, smelled the intoxicating scent of his skin. Her nipples hardened, tingling for the touch of his hands, his mouth; between her legs flowed a honeyed warmth and an aching need to be filled.

His fingers slipped beneath the wide, scooped neckline of her muumuu and cupped her swollen naked flesh. Electricity flashed from her nipples to her loins.

Cole's mouth hovered a fraction above her lips. "Chelsea, I promised myself that I wasn't going to rush you into bed again, that I'd let you set whatever limits you feel you need. But stop me now if you're going to, because if you don't, we'll be spending the day in bed."

For a moment, Chelsea went limp against him, leaning her head against his chest and letting his hard muscular frame support her. She was weak and pliant and aroused. She wanted nothing more than for him to push her down onto the bed and make love to her. She wanted to be swept away, to not have to think, or make sensible decisions or take responsibility...

But Cole had given her the power to make her own choice, to take control of the situation. Vaguely, she recalled she'd wanted that power. Cole continued to hold her, making no demands or further attempts to arouse her. Slowly, her head stopped spinning, but her body still raged with unsatisfied passion, which quickly turned to frustration mixed with irritation.

Why did Cole have to choose right now to go noble on her? she thought testily. In a way, he was still calling all the shots because only his self-control had given her this chance to be in charge; hers was nonexistent and they both knew it. It was a humbling admission.

She pulled herself out of his arms. Common sense told her that it would be a mistake to fall into bed with Cole when so much was still unresolved between them. She sighed with a mingling of resignation and regret. Common sense could be so prosaic, and her feelings for Cole were anything but.

"Not going to let sex cloud your judgment, hmm?" Cole asked dryly, but the hard intensity of his gaze belied the lightness of his tone.

"We already know that sex between us is good, but a relationship can't be based solely on sex. We can't spend our whole lives in bed—there has to be something else. Mutual respect and trust and—"

"Love," he finished. "We have that, Chelsea." Their eyes met and held. "And the respect, too. Maybe we need a little work in the trust department, but we'll get there, sweetheart." He reached out and cupped her cheek with his hand.

"How can you be so sure?" she whispered. Cole never had doubts or uncertainties; he never wasted time second-guessing himself. When he wanted something he went after it while she . . .

Chelsea sighed again. She vacillated back and forth, driving herself crazy. Perhaps this was all because she'd been raised by two people who hated each other. She had loved them both and was forever bouncing from one side to the other.

"I think we're definitely making progress, Chelsea." Cole smiled. "Instead of telling me how obstinate, headstrong and intractable I am, you're asking me how I can be sure. Let me demonstrate why I'm so sure. Have dinner with me tonight."

She thought it over. He would take her to an expensive, luxuriously appointed restaurant with romantic ambience, fine wine and marvelous food. He would be charming and attentive and when he took her in his arms at the end of the evening, she would be so completely under his spell that she could never be able to summon the willpower and the stamina to say no to him, not even if he gallantly gave her time to consider. She loved him too much, she wanted him too much.

Chelsea raised her chin and tightened her lips into a straight line. None of that had anything to do with building trust. And...she hadn't truly forgiven him for the things he'd said yesterday, Chelsea admitted silently. She may as well be honest with herself, part of her wanted to punish him some more. She didn't want to make it too easy for him to get her back.

So she'd better say no to him while she still could. She straightened her shoulders and lifted her chin resolutely. "No thank you, Cole. I—have things to do tonight."

"Mmm, I'm sure you have a full schedule. Washing your hair, doing your laundry, worrying about Stefanie. And let's not forget your top priority, punishing Cole Tremaine. Driving him even crazier than he is. That's undoubtedly at the head of your list."

"Let me get this straight. You're going to give me the time and the space I need, you're going to let me set the limits, but whenever I attempt to do that, you're going to have a tantrum and sulk."

"I don't have tantrums and I never sulk," Cole said loftily. "I'm simply—disappointed I won't be seeing you tonight."

Chelsea bit back a smile. Cole Tremaine attempting the art of compromise was a sight seldom seen. But she didn't want it all her way, either. "Maybe you could call me tonight?" she suggested hesitantly.

"I'll do that." He smiled thinly, then glanced at his watch. "I have a meeting in less than an hour. I'd better head back to the office, Chelsea." He reached for her again and kissed her, hard, then stalked from the apartment.

A meeting. Chelsea frowned. She remembered what he'd said about spending the day in bed with her. There had been no mention of a meeting then. Would he have canceled it, if she'd succumbed to his lovemaking? Or was this alleged meeting simply a convenient excuse for him to leave her because she hadn't hopped into bed with him?"

She thought about what he'd said, that the trusting side of their relationship needed work. Trust wouldn't grow if she kept attributing ambiguous ulterior motives to his actions. She should take his words at face value, not assume he was trying to manipulate her. If she wanted things to work out between them...

If? Who was she kidding? Chelsea asked herself wryly. She most definitely wanted everything to work out. She wanted a full-fledged happy ending and beyond for her and Cole. That meant she must stop doubting him and begin believing what he told her. From "I love you" to "I have a meeting."

It might not be easy, but as Cole had pointed out, this relationship of theirs had never been easy. Maybe it was better that way. With their backgrounds they needed to learn from the start that love often wasn't easy, but that it could prevail if both partners cared enough—and could trust each other.

The *Capitol Scene* staff's reaction to Chelsea's appearance at the office later that day ranged from astonishment to awkwardness, with a bit of embarrassment thrown in on all sides. The last time anyone had seen her had been at the going-away party the staff had thrown for her.

But everybody politely kept their curiosity under wraps and assiduously avoided the subject. Only one, Al Donovan, the magazine's managing editor, asked her frankly, "What the hell happened, Chelsea?"

She swallowed, shrugged and tried to appear insouciant. "It just didn't work out, Al. It wasn't meant to be."

"Bull," he said bluntly. "So who dumped who?"

Chelsea winced. "Will you buy a—uh—mutual dump?"

"Hell, no. I'm hearing rumors that Strickland is on the verge of eloping with another woman. That he's really hot for his new babe and wants to marry her immediately, without any of that First Wedding garbage."

First Wedding garbage? Chelsea almost laughed. As if all of it hadn't been instigated by the Stricklands in the first place! But the knowledge that Seth's "new babe" was her poor misguided little sister Stefanie effectively quashed her laughter.

"Are you going to write an exclusive story about the big bust-up for us, Chelsea?" Al asked hopefully.

"Al, do you know that you have a clone working for the *Globe Star Probe*?" she asked with acid sweetness. "His name is Kaufman and you two will have to get together soon. You have so much in common."

Al scowled ferociously and dropped his inquisition. "Well, since you're back and not working on anything specific at the moment, you can help Mark Masloff with the movie reviews. With the glut of new summer releases, he's fallen a bit behind and needs someone to pick up the slack."

This was Al's revenge for her *Globe Star Probe* crack, Chelsea knew. Masloff, the magazine's movie critic, jealously guarded his turf, giving only the most abominable films to the others to review.

"*Prom Night at Horror High: The Sequel* is opening today. If you hurry, you can make the one o'clock show," continued Al. "Have the review in ASAP."

Chelsea groaned. "They made a sequel to *Prom Night at Horror High*?" She'd had to review that one; abominable was a bit too complimentary a term for it.

"It was a box office smash," Al said snidely. "Enjoy the show, Chelsea."

She didn't. The sequel was as repulsive as its predecessor, and she was back at her desk working on her review when her phone rang.

"How was the latest dismemberment flick?" Cole's voice, droll with humor, came over the line.

"I'm searching my thesaurus for synonyms for revolting. If there is a *Prom Night at Horror High III*, I'm not going to review it."

"I called earlier and was told you were on assignment. Chelsea, about tonight... I know you're busy..."

There was a pause. He waited for her to tell him that she'd changed her mind and would spend the evening with him. She waited for him to insist that she change her mind and spend the evening with him.

Silence prevailed on both ends of the line.

Cole spoke first. "Since you have plans of your own tonight, I'm sure you won't mind if I make some plans myself."

"Of course not," she said bracingly. "We're both independent adults, Cole. There is no reason for us to have to check in with the other."

"I want you to check in with me, baby. I want to know where you are and who you're with. I'd like you to have the same information about me, too."

Possessive, but reasonable, Chelsea decided. She liked that. Especially since she felt the same way. "I'm spending the evening in my apartment, Cole. I want to finish up this review and call Stefanie, make a few more calls to some friends to explain why I'm not on my honeymoon and then go to bed early. I've very tired. I had less than five hours sleep last night."

"And you assume that you wouldn't get much sleep if I were in your bed?"

Chelsea actually blushed. "I—"

"I realize that I can be relentless at times. But so can you, darling." She drew a sharp, audible breath and Cole laughed. "And it's unfair of me to tease you over the phone, isn't it, pet? I can picture you sitting at your desk blushing while trying to pretend this is a professional call."

"You're a bit of a fiend, Cole Tremaine," she said softly.

He chuckled again. "Chelsea, I'll be having dinner at the Four Seasons tonight, with Carling Templeton and her parents and some friends from their hometown in Texas."

Chelsea's fingers seemed to turn to ice as she clutched the receiver. "What?" Didn't he realize that his punishment was to be deprived of her company this evening? It did not include alternative companions.

"Carling called me this afternoon and asked if I'd join her. Her parents are entertaining two couples, longtime friends of theirs, and she needed an escort."

"And you told her you'd go?" His actions smacked of betrayal and jealousy seared her like a scorching flame. *A bit of a fiend?* she'd said teasingly. Not exactly. His cozy little dinner date with Carling advanced him to the full-fledged fiend category.

"I told Carling I had to check my schedule and I'd get back to her," Cole continued smoothly. "But as long as you and I aren't doing anything, I might as well go with her. I enjoy the Four Seasons and I like the Templetons."

From his point of view, there really was no reason why he shouldn't, and the rational side of her accepted this. But the emotional, possessive, passionate side of her churned in turmoil. Cole might think that his relationship with Carling Templeton was platonic, but Chelsea didn't believe for one minute that the gorgeous, sophisticated senator's daughter wasn't trying to sink her treacherous hooks into him. That story about her father trying to match her up with a reclusive rancher sounded like a tall tale to Chelsea. She didn't even believe there was such a rancher. He was a myth, a ploy to lure an unsuspecting Cole to her cool blond web!

Cole is mine! she cried in silent fury. She did not want him wining and dining another woman under any circumstances, particularly not a beautiful, charming one like Carling Templeton! Worse, he'd just admitted that he *wanted* to go.

"What kind of a whirlwind courtship is this, anyway?" Chelsea was horrified to hear herself ask the question. But once she started, she couldn't seem to stop. "You're going out with another woman while I—"

"Chelsea, you told me you didn't want to see me tonight," he interjected with maddening patience.

"So you have to go out and paint the town with *her*? Is it mandatory for you to spend every evening with a woman—any woman? What's wrong with you spending a quiet evening at your place? Alone! Don't you have phone calls to make and correspondence to catch up on and things like laundry to do?"

"No. I have a staff that attends to all of that for me." On his end of the line, Cole was smiling broadly. "Chelsea, if you don't want me to have dinner with Carling and the others, just say so. I won't go if it upsets you."

Wasn't he telling her exactly what she wanted to hear? Chelsea asked herself. The answer was a resounding no! "You want to go!" she accused. "You like Carling and the Templetons and the Four Seasons. You admitted it."

"That's true. But if you don't want me to go, I won't. I'll call Carling and tell her I can't make it."

"No!" That wasn't good enough, she fumed. She wanted him to say that he'd rather vacation in war-torn Lebanon than spend one minute in the loathsome company of Carling and the Templetons. She wanted him to say that a dinner at the Four Seasons was conducive to food poisoning and he had no desire to set foot in the place. Without her. She wanted him to tell her that he was willing to quietly stay put when she decided she had other things to do. And she wanted him to *mean* it!

She knew she was being irrational. Cole seemed to inspire her to carry on like a raving lunatic. But she made an effort to at least masquerade as a rational being. "There's no reason for you not to go. I'm busy and we're both independent adults, free to do as we please." She gritted her teeth. That it was true didn't mean she had to like it. "I hope you enjoy yourself."

"You do trust me, don't you, Chelsea?" His voice was low and intense. "You know I have no sexual interest in Carling. The only woman I want is you. If you have any doubts about that, if my going to dinner with Carling causes you to distrust me, I won't go."

Now she was backed into a corner, Chelsea thought grimly. The odd thing was that she did trust Cole not to end the evening in bed with Carling. But how could she tell him that the thought of him even sharing a table with the cool blond beauty disturbed her? She'd sound like an unreasonably possessive paranoid and she didn't care for the image.

It was just that she didn't want Cole to be viewed as a free agent, as an eligible bachelor, fair game for any woman in Washington. Because he belonged to her, just as much as she belonged to him. Despite the hurt and the misunderstandings in the past, she was ready to commit herself to him again. She was also ready to stop punishing him for what had gone wrong in the mountains. Maybe he'd been punishing her for four years ago. Maybe he had unwittingly driven her to abandon him in a sad, subconscious reenactment of losing his mother's love.

Still, it was all behind them now. In punishing her, Cole had admitted punishing himself just as painfully. If he'd driven her away, he'd come back, determined to claim her again. It was time to shake off the past and move ahead.

"Honey, I've got a call on another line." Cole was suddenly all brisk businessman. "I'll talk to you tomorrow."

He hung up, and she sat staring at the receiver. Foiled by Call Waiting. She hadn't had the chance to tell him of her newfound insights and perceptions. She was certain that this was one armchair analysis he'd have welcomed hearing.

Chelsea was tempted to call him back, to tell him that she was claiming him for this evening and every other evening from now on. But Al called an unscheduled staff meeting and she had to go to it.

"Before we start, I have some good news to share," Al said, opening the meeting. "Word has just come down that the Tremaine drugstore chain has requested distribution of *Capitol Scene* to all their stores, to commence immediately. They also want *Capitol Scene* in all their bookstores. Not just in the D.C. area, but nationally!"

There was a spontaneous round of applause from the staffers gathered in the conference room.

"I never could figure out why we were cut from the Tremaine stores," Al muttered, shaking his head. "Well, for whatever reason, we're back in and I don't have to tell you what a substantial circulation boost this gives the magazine."

Chelsea didn't doubt for a moment that Cole was responsible for the decision. She understood the message he was sending: he supported her career and would do whatever he could to help her. *Capitol Scene* was no longer his enemy, standing in the way of his plans for her. The punishment was truly over for both of them.

After the initial euphoria of Al's announcement faded, the meeting dragged on interminably for Chelsea. All she could think of was Cole; she *had* to talk to him.

She tried to call him at his Tremaine Incorporated office before she left work, but he was en route to a meeting and couldn't be reached. And when she tried to call him at home, she was told by the no-nonsense directory assistance operator that Cole Tremaine's home phone number was unlisted. He'd moved from his apartment to an expensive condominium three years ago and his phone number had changed along with his address. She had no way of getting in touch with him tonight—unless he called her.

Of course she could always have him paged at the Four Seasons restaurant...it was an incredibly appealing thought but Chelsea decided against it. She would spend this evening as she'd originally planned. Carling Templeton could borrow Cole this one final time and then she was on her own. Let her find some other knight to protect her from that boogeyman, the mythical rancher.

She had just popped a frozen package of chicken à la king in the microwave when her doorbell rang. She ran to answer it, thinking for one heart-stopping moment that Cole had changed his plans. She imagined him grabbing her into his arms and...

Eleven

Her fantasy died an instant death. Kieran Kaufman and Miles Rodgers were at the door. "Oh, it's you."

Kaufman shrugged. "Well, that's a better reception than we usually get from people. At least you didn't scream, curse and slam the door in our faces."

"We're here to give you these," Miles shoved a rather bedraggled half dozen white carnations into her hand. "In thanks for resurrecting our careers."

Chelsea stared at the carnations, long past their floral prime. "Uh, thanks."

"We thought about getting you roses," Kaufman interjected. "But we're too cheap. I bargained a street vendor down to a buck fifty for these." He pushed his way inside her apartment, saw the roses that filled it and shrugged. "Jeez, am I glad we didn't spring for the roses! You've got enough here to open your own shop. I take it you and Tremaine have patched things up?"

"Well, sort of," she admitted. If she'd been able to talk to Cole this afternoon, she could have given a qualified yes as an answer.

"Is he here?" Miles asked curiously.

She shook her head. "He's—having dinner with Carling Templeton." For the life of her, she couldn't figure out why she was confiding in this pair, except that they'd already been around for some of the worst scenes of her life. It hardly seemed worth trying to keep up an image with them now.

Kaufman gave a low whistle. "He's with the Ice Princess? Well, I guess you have no worries there. No guy would give up a hot-blooded babe like you for Glacier Woman."

"I never thought I'd take kindly to being called a hot-blooded babe but in this context, I thank you," Chelsea said dryly.

"Yeah, Darling Caring is a cold one. We're talking arctic." Kaufman walked over to the television set and turned it on. "We want to watch this with you...the interview that catapulted us from the *Globe Star Probe* to Channel Seven in D.C."

"All three networks bought clips of our interview with Stefanie," Rodgers exclaimed excitedly. "CNN bought the entire tape. Channel Seven was so impressed—with us and our connections—that we were both hired this afternoon."

"Your connections?" Chelsea echoed.

Kaufman nodded. "The Stricklands were so delighted with our interview that they told us they would be indebted to us. *Indebted*, Chelsea. You know what that means? We've got an inside track to the White House."

Chelsea sank down onto the couch. "It also means that you coached Stefanie in that interview. That it wasn't the disaster I was counting on."

"It would've been," said Miles. "We couldn't believe the way she went on and on about—"

"I know, I know. I talked to her, too, remember?" Chelsea interrupted, sighing. "But you didn't get it on tape?"

"Not on your life, babe," said Kaufman. "We wanted the Stricklands to look kindly on us. We wanted them to feel indebted to us. So we fed little Stefanie all the right things to say. About her and Seth falling madly in love and struggling to conceal their feelings because they didn't want to hurt the bride-to-be. You."

"Look, it's on!" cried Miles, pointing to the screen.

They watched Stefanie, pretty and demure in a white sundress, her long blond hair arranged artfully over her shoulders, talking all about her overwhelming passion for Seth Strickland and her hopes that her older sister Chelsea would find it in her heart to forgive them and go on to make a new life for herself. Breathlessly, her big dark eyes shining, she confided her fondest wish, to be a good wife to Seth and make a happy marriage.

"An impressive performance," Chelsea murmured. Kaufman and Rodgers were equally impressive in their roles as serious journalists.

"It's the lead on all three networks!" exulted Kaufman. "We've scooped America! We've scooped the world!"

"I hope you don't mind that we sort of made it sound like Strickland dumped you for Stefanie, Chelsea," Miles offered apologetically. "Now you've got the public image of a reject, but it played better than Seth asking Stefanie to marry him to pump up his ego and her agreeing because she wanted fame and fortune."

"No one can resist a love story," Kieran added with his usual sardonic leer. "All the world loves lovers, so they say."

"I don't care about my pubic image," said Chelsea with a troubled frown. "I just don't want my little sister stuck in a miserable, loveless marriage."

"Hey, don't worry about it, babe." Kieran Kaufman gave her shoulder an encouraging pat. "If ever there were two people who deserved each other, it's your sister and Seth Strickland. And on that note, we're outta here. We've got a lot of calls to return, huh, Miles?"

Miles nodded happily. "We owe it all to you, Chelsea. Keep in touch."

Her own phone began to ring a few minutes after Stefanie's appearance on the nightly news with calls from friends and relatives, neighbors, co-workers, acquaintances, new and old. Even her second-grade teacher phoned, all to offer her support and encouragement in these difficult times. When the media calls for interviews began to come in, she unplugged her phone from its jack, undressed and went to bed. What a relief it was going to be when she was no longer newsworthy!

When her doorbell rang at ten o'clock, Chelsea was certain it was Cole. She hopped out of bed and ran to the door, not bothering to put anything over her lilac teddy, which had been a shower gift from her stepmother. Gifts of clothing from her family were the only engagement and wedding presents she'd allowed herself to keep; everything else was being returned to the donors, courtesy of the Strickland staff.

She imagined Cole's reaction when he saw the sexy, skimpy garment and her heart skipped at least three beats.

She flung open the door. Another fantasy came to an abrupt end; hers were dropping like flies in a cloud of insect repellent tonight. "Hi, Stef." She greeted her sister with something less than enthusiasm.

"You're expecting Cole Tremaine I see," Stefanie surmised, her dark eyes sweeping over her older sister.

Chelsea stepped aside and let her in. "How did you know that Cole and I are—"

"Back together, hotter and heavier than ever?" Stefanie finished for her. "No, I'm not psychic. All the phone calls and commotion last night were a clue, but when Cole called me this afternoon and offered me double the amount the

Stricklands gave me if I wouldn't go through with my plans to marry Seth, I knew you were practically Mrs. Cole Tremaine. So when exactly is your wedding?"

Chelsea's eyes widened. "Cole offered you money not to marry Seth?"

"I'm not for sale, Chelsea," Stefanie said, sounding rather disgruntled. "I'm not quite *that* shallow. I really do want to marry Seth. I can't wait to be Stefanie Strickland."

"Steffie, I saw you on the news tonight, you don't have to reenact it for me now. If they gave Oscars for interviews, you'd win best actress and Kaufman and Rodgers would walk away with writing and directing awards."

Stefanie smiled. "They were wonderful, Chelsea. They told me just what to say and how to say it. They even let the Stricklands preview the tape. Thanks so much for sending them over."

"Stefanie, I didn't do it as a favor. I don't want you to marry Seth."

"I know." Stefanie sighed. "Cole told me that you were worried about me, that's why he tried to bribe me not to go through with it. I appreciate your concern, both yours and Cole's, but I want to be rich *and* famous. Marrying Seth will make me both."

"And you came all the way over here tonight to tell me that?"

"I've been trying to call you for hours, but I couldn't get through. I had to talk to you, Chelsea. I wanted to thank you for having Cole offer me the money. I know you meant well, and I—I wanted to make sure you weren't mad at me for the interview and all. I know you dumped Seth and not the other way around, and I hate having everybody think you were the one who got rejected."

"That's very loyal of you, Stefanie." Chelsea put her arm around her sister's shoulders and gave her a quick hug. "I'm not mad at you, but I still wish you'd reconsider this whole marriage."

"Never!" She clutched Chelsea's hand. "But I couldn't stand it if you hated me, Chelsea. You've always been there for me. I think you're the only person in the world who I really do love."

"Oh, Stefanie!" Chelsea felt tears well in her eyes. The travails of their miserable, embattled childhood had left them both with emotional scars, but Stefanie's were deeper and with more dire consequences. Chelsea had opened herself to the healing power of a loving, intimate relationship; Stefanie refused to take that risk.

The more Stefanie talked about her arid future with Seth Strickland, the more Chelsea longed to be with Cole. She wanted to thank him for everything he'd done for her today—from lifting the ban on *Capitol Scene* to trying to buy off Stefanie to spare her from worrying. Yes, she'd definitely had all the time and space she needed. Had they had the shortest whirlwind courtship on record—one that had begun a day or so ago—or the longest, begun four years ago? It didn't really matter. The idea of rushing into marriage held an irresistible appeal. She wanted to tell Cole so.

Stefanie stayed talking till midnight, and by then Chelsea was so exhausted that she decided not to risk the late-night drive to Cole's condo on the other side of the beltway. She would get up early and catch him before he left for the office. She smiled as she thought of surprising him; maybe neither one of them would make it to their respective offices at all!

She arrived at Cole's the next morning later than she'd planned. First, she'd slept through her alarm. Next, she'd learned that there would be no "squalling bundle of joy" following their careless night—and morning—of passion. She was disappointed. Though she'd been certain the timing was wrong for a pregnancy, she realized that she wanted to have Cole's baby ASAP, as the *Capitol Scene* editors were always saying. As soon as possible.

She sighed with longing and muted disappointment. It looked as if she and Cole would be spending the day at their offices rather than making love. Well, there would be other times.

She swung by his condominium, her anticipation rising. She couldn't wait to see Cole. The future had never looked brighter. Together, she and Cole could handle anything, she decided happily. They would overcome whatever problems and obstacles and emerge all the stronger and more secure in their love. Even coping with the prospect of Stefanie's certain eventual misery would be eased having Cole by her side.

Chelsea pulled her car into a parking space and hurried along the sidewalk, remembering the first time she had come here three years ago, right after she'd learned he had moved. She had found out his new address and driven by because she had to know where he was, where to find him. It occurred to her that he'd done the same thing with her. Fining out where she lived, keeping track of her dates and her work on *Capitol Scene*.

They might have been separated for the past four years, but the ties between them had never really been broken. They were truly destined to be together. Her eyes misted with tears.

She was blinking them away when she saw Cole emerge from the front door of his condo, his hand cupping the elbow of a slender, shapely young woman with long pale blond hair who was wearing a trendy short, strapless jade evening dress and very high heels. She wore no stockings and no makeup.

Chelsea stopped dead in her tracks. She recognized the woman immediately. She was Carling Templeton. And she looked tousled and sexy and not a bit like a glacier woman or an ice princess.

Cole and Carling came to a halt, too. For one interminable, ridiculous moment, the three of them stood in shocked silence facing each other in the middle of Cole's front walk.

Carling recovered first. "Oh, you're Chelsea!" she exclaimed, reaching out to lay her hand on Chelsea's forearm. "Please, you have to believe that this isn't what it looks like at all!"

Chelsea carefully eased her arm away. "It looks like you spent the night here," she said in a clear, calm voice. The woman's attire left no doubt about it. Chelsea's eyes flicked to Cole who was clean-shaven, impeccably groomed, and dressed for the office in a summerweight tan suit. He, at least, wasn't wearing yesterday's clothes.

"I spent the night here but I didn't *spend the night* here!" cried Carling, blushing. "Do you understand what I mean?"

Chelsea was transfixed by her blush. It covered all of her bare skin and there was a lot of that. "No," she said flatly.

"She means we didn't sleep together," Cole put in roughly. His face was as pale as Carling's was crimson. "I swear it's the truth, Chelsea."

Chelsea folded her arms in front of her and stared at him. He was beginning to perspire and his hands were clenched into fists, so tightly that his knuckles had whitened. "I see," she said.

"Cole is a wonderful man!" cried Carling. "He loves you and he would never do anything to jeopardize your relationship. You have to believe that, Chelsea!" Again, she clutched at Chelsea's arm.

Chelsea resisted the urge to swat her away like a mosquito. She took a few steps back from her instead. "Did you try to get him to do something to jeopardize our relationship, Carling?" she asked severely.

Carling vigorously shook her head no.

"Chelsea, last night we went to dinner, just as I told you we were going to," Cole said urgently.

"And he ordered a bottle of champagne and announced to our table that he was getting married," Carling cut in tearfully. She gazed at Chelsea with watery blue eyes. "To you."

Chelsea's eyes flew to Cole's face. "You did?" she whispered.

"I did. Maybe I jumped the gun a little but I wanted it to be true more than anything in the world, Chelsea." Cole took both hands in his. "Will you marry me, my darling? On whatever date you choose?"

She didn't pull away. This didn't seem like the right time to remind him that he'd said he would never propose to her again, that it was her turn to do the proposing. But it was definitely the right time to prove to him that she trusted him absolutely, that however damning the circumstantial evidence, she believed in him and his love for her.

Cole loved her too much to risk damaging the trust they were rebuilding together for a night in the sack with Carling Templeton. She had never been more sure of anything in her life.

"Yes, Cole," she said softly and moved close to him. "I love you. There's nothing I want more than to be your wife. ASAP," she added, smiling up at him, her dark eyes glowing.

His arms went around her and he hugged her so tightly she almost couldn't breathe. But she didn't mind for she was holding on to him just as tight, clinging to him possessively.

"Sweetheart, you've made me the happiest man in the world," he said huskily, kissing her, caressing her with his big, warm hands. "I feel as if I've gone from hell to heaven in the span of two minutes! When I saw you coming up the walk, I was terrified you'd assume the worst and never forgive me. Chelsea, I've never loved anyone as much as I love you and I never will. You mean everything to me."

"I know," she said simply. "It's the same with me." She cocked her head toward Carling who managed a quavering smile. Chelsea didn't feel quite up to smiling back. "What about you?" she asked. "How did you end up here all night?"

"There was a terrible scene with my father when we got home from the restaurant," Carling said quietly, holding Chelsea's gaze. "Daddy wasn't at all happy with the news of Cole's engagement. He accused me of 'letting another live one get away' as he put it. I've always been the apple of Daddy's eye and it hurt so much to have him disappointed in me. He started threatening me with that rancher again—"

"There really is a rancher?" Chelsea interrupted incredulously.

Carling shuddered. "I don't care if Daddy disowns me. I will not marry that man!" She started to cry again. "After Daddy and Mother went to bed I started drinking. I just wanted to forget the whole dreadful scene, to pass out in bed except it didn't work out that way. I got more and more agitated instead. Without really thinking about what I was doing, I drove over here and Cole let me inside. He lectured me for driving drunk and then ordered me into one of the guest rooms for the night. Then I passed out. I woke up this morning feeling pretty sick. I probably look like the specter of death."

"Well, not quite that bad," Chelsea conceded, feeling a bit more generous toward her.

"I can drive myself home, now." Carling glanced from Chelsea to Cole. "I know you two want to be alone."

"We certainly do," Cole said eagerly and scooped Chelsea up into his arms. He carried her into the condo without a backward glance at Carling who was walking, her shoulders drooping, toward her car, a sporty little red Miata. Chelsea was unable to resist stealing a quick peek at her.

"I think I feel sorry for Carling," she said as Cole sat down in a big leather winged chair, holding her on his lap. "Her father sounds like some kind of awful medieval tyrant."

"No, honey, just a politician accustomed to getting his way."

"Poor Carling. And there really *is* a rancher!"

"Of course there is. That's why I was going out with her."

"For a smooth operator, you can be very naive," Chelsea said, indulgent in her womanly wisdom. "You need me around to make sure no one takes advantage of your chivalrous nature."

"I need you around, period." He curved his hand around her neck and drew her closer, brushing his lips slowly back and forth over hers. Then his tongue slid into her mouth and he kissed her deeply, rapaciously with all the love and passion that he felt for her. And would always feel.

His fingers went to the bodice of her dress and he began to unbutton it. She was wearing a snowy white camisole and his thumb flicked over her tightly distended nipple. "I want you to have my children. As many as you want, whenever you want to have them."

He spread one hand wide over the smooth curve of her stomach. "I want to see your body round and filled with my child." And slipped his other hand under the smooth silk and cupped her warm breast. "And I want to watch you feed our babies."

"I want that too, Cole," she whispered, pressing her hands over his. "And I want a baby right away." She blushed a little. "I'm just sorry that I'm not pregnant right now."

His eyes narrowed perceptively. "I think I'm glad, especially after what happened at the cottage afterward. I don't want you to associate the conception of our child with anything but love and pleasure."

"Not to mention that it's not only irresponsible and harebrained for a man who is nearly thirty-five years old to get a woman pregnant out of wedlock. It's downright tacky," she teased, rubbing her lips against his neck.

"Mmm, not to mention that."

They laughed and kissed and soon their laughter had stilled and they were kissing with increasing ardor. When they finally, reluctantly broke apart, Chelsea gazed at him with dark velvety eyes filled with emotion.

"When I think of how close we came to almost losing each other..." She shivered and snuggled closer, stroking his face, his hair, his neck as if to reassure herself that he was really here with her. "Cole, what if you hadn't come by my apartment the morning of the wedding and followed me out of town? What if I'd decided not to call off my wedding to Seth?"

Cole smiled with lazy confidence. "If you hadn't called off the wedding, I'd probably be facing federal kidnapping charges because I know now there is no way I would have let you marry Strickland. It was a fait accompli the moment I decided to drive by your apartment that morning. Of course, you might have been a bit irked with my domineering interference in your life, but—" he shrugged. "—I'd have held you hostage in the mountains and clouded your judgment with sex until—"

"I was sufficiently docile and submissive?" Chelsea interrupted mischievously. "Do you still want me as my feisty, outspoken self?"

"I'll take you any way I can have you," he said fervidly. Then he grinned. "Anyway, I'd worry that you were coming down with a virus or something if you ever became too docile. I love you just the way you are, Chelsea," he added, tucking a strand of her hair behind her ear in a loving, possessive gesture. "I fell in love with you the moment I saw you. You're my obsession and I wouldn't have it any other way."

"I feel the same way about you," Chelsea said, adoring him while basking in his adoration. "Our whirlwind courtship is going to evolve into a lifelong marriage."

"Beginning ASAP," agreed Cole, taking her mouth in a passionate kiss.

Epilogue

Exactly ten months later, Chelsea woke her husband at midnight to announce, "It's time." The gentle April shower that had begun earlier in the evening had escalated to a torrential downpour. Traffic on the beltway was heavy and backed up even at that late hour. And Cole's car stalled twice along the way. Despite his terror that she would have the baby in the car and he would have to deliver it, they made it to the hospital in plenty of time for eight-pound Daniel Richard Tremaine's appearance at four a.m.

They had taken natural childbirth classes together and Cole acted as Chelsea's coach during labor, encouraging her all the way. Cole stared at his wife and his hour-old son, his eyes filled with awe and wonder as dark-haired little Daniel nuzzled at his mother's breast.

"He's really here," Cole marveled, laying his finger in the newborn's palm. The infant's tiny fingers closed around it in a reflexive fist. "An hour ago, he was inside you and now he's here... I can't believe it."

"I can," Chelsea said fervently. "Having gone through labor and delivery, I find it entirely believable!" She cuddled her son and smiled up at her husband. "You did a great job, coach. I couldn't have done it without you."

"You did all the work. Ah, Chelsea, I thought our wedding day was the happiest day of my life, but today ranks right up there with it."

"For me, too," Chelsea said softly.

She couldn't wait to take the baby home and begin their lives together as a family. She was free-lancing now, working at home for *Capitol Scene* and various other publications. She had resigned from full-time employment in her later months of pregnancy and loved the independence and freedom free-lance writing permitted. It was a good way to keep herself creatively occupied while raising a family. She had the best of both worlds and it had been her own choice. There had been no decrees from Cole. Their marriage didn't operate that way.

The past ten months brought interesting changes in other lives, too.

Stefanie Strickland, wife of Seth, had become a national media star, her unique blend of sultry wholesomeness gracing magazine covers across the land. She worked tirelessly on behalf of the Strickland White House; whatever the event, important or trivial, if there were still or video cameras present, Stefanie was there. Her collection of First Family photographs, published in hardcover, was selling briskly. She'd framed the newspaper article that called her "America's Answer to Princess Diana."

Miles Rodgers was named White House correspondent by the network; his close ties to the Stricklands—he was rumored to be Stefanie's particular confidant—made him an invaluable source.

Senator Clayton Templeton and his wife announced the engagement of their daughter Carling to Kane McClellan, a West Texas rancher.

Kieran Kaufman was back at the *Globe Star Probe*. He claimed he'd left Channel Seven because the *Probe* made him an offer he couldn't refuse. Channel Seven insisted they'd fired him for sleaziness unbecoming one of their employees.

And on the checkout stands, the *Globe Star Probe* reported that Big Foot had been sighted frolicking with the Loch Ness Monster in the wilds of Scotland. Kaufman had even obtained exclusive photos....

* * * * *